Carrie Y. Hargreaves

Poste Restante

A Novel: Vol. I

Carrie Y. Hargreaves

Poste Restante
A Novel: Vol. I

ISBN/EAN: 9783337064921

Printed in Europe, USA, Canada, Australia, Japan

Cover: Foto ©Andreas Hilbeck / pixelio.de

More available books at **www.hansebooks.com**

POSTE RESTANTE

A Novel

BY

C. Y. HARGREAVES

AUTHOR OF 'PAUL ROMER'

IN THREE VOLUMES

VOL. I

LONDON
ADAM AND CHARLES BLACK
1894

DEDICATED

TO MY DEAR MOTHER

CONTENTS

CHAPTER I

Heaven from all creatures hides the book of fate.

POPE.

ONE—two—three—four! With a resonant
boom the big bronze giants on the clock
tower hammered out the flight of time : then
the echoes died away, and the clatter of feet
and the noisy hum of voices rose again in the
Piazza San Marco. The afternoon siesta was
over, and Venice had awakened. In the
grand square, where the heart of the city
beats, all was life,—lazy, languid life, if you
like; for it is there in the piazza where
Italian, French, Greek, German, English
nationalities meet in one common whole, and
discuss their caffé, or ices, or aniseed water
with cosmopolitan friendliness.

There was the usual crowd of loiterers
thronging the chairs before Florian's caffé;
the usual beggars grouped in the centre
of the piazza and before the entrance to
the great Cathedral itself; the usual pro-
menaders sauntering along under the old and
new Procuratie, or wending their way through
the narrow entrance of the Merceria. The
pigeons were fluttering about—a mass of soft
gray feathers—as they chirped and scrambled
and hopped inquisitively amongst the idlers.
It was the same fifty years ago; it will be
the same fifty years hence. Venice, bereft
of her Piazza San Marco, would be as the
play of *Hamlet* with the Prince of Denmark
left out.

If you are bored and want amusement, you
go to the piazza; if you are a bird of passage,
with only a few hours to spare, you go to the
piazza; if you are a resident, still you go to
the piazza. It is here where the soul of
Venice has her being, here where her pulse
throbs, here where all the fascination of that

beautiful city contracts as in a common focus. You may wander to the Mole and gaze interestedly upon the shipping; you may stroll along the Riva degli Schiavoni finding amusement in its life and chatter, but, as the day draws on, so as surely are you drawn back to the piazza, to linger there in idle content and sip your favourite drink.

It was just as the clock chimed out the hour of four, one lazy, sunny afternoon in May, that a young man sauntered across the piazza from amongst one of the groups of idlers, and stood hesitating for a moment at the entrance to the Merceria. It was but a second, to answer a jest from some Italian officer lounging there, and to refuse with a laughing shake of the head the invitation to coffee, which he would have liked to accept; and then he turned into the Merceria, where his rate of speed was checked or modified by the crowds of people thronging the narrow tortuous street, which is to Venice what Regent Street is to London, or the Corso to

Rome, and where all the youth and beauty
of this silent city on the sea pursue the
avocation dear to the feminine heart,—of
shopping.

A little later and he paused again, this
time upon a bridge spanning one of the side
canals, and looked down with a sort of absent
curiosity at the gondoliers, forcing their craft
with such dexterity through the sluggish
waters; then went on more slowly still, not
exactly now by reason of the crowd, but
rather as if that momentary check had turned
his thoughts into a different channel, which
culminated in a reverie so profound that
more by instinct than actual effort he at last
drifted into the Post Office, and made his way
to the *Poste Restante* department.

This reverie—a pleasant one, to judge by
the smile which brightened his features—held
possession of him even after he had presented
his card to the clerk and waited for his letters.

As he stood there, one hand leaning lightly
upon the ledge, an onlooker might have been

puzzled to determine which country had given him birth. The eyes, of a bluish gray, soft and dark in some lights, quick and full of mirth in others, were Irish by shape and colour, but the contour of the face, long and inclining to oval, lacked Hibernian breadth and squareness. The shrewd, clear-cut lines of mouth and chin were undeniably English ; but again, as if in direct contradiction to this, the bright brown wavy hair was worn longer than is customary with the young male Briton, and allowed to curl as nature willed it about the head. His dress was artistic, even a little Bohemian, with a gay-coloured sash worn in lieu of a waistcoat, and a slouching gray felt hat overshadowing his features. There was a careless, but by no means un-tidy negligence about the whole get-up, which spoke more of the man of Art than Science—a vivid, even daring blending of colour, foreign to English notions and English tastes. An attractive man, most women would have said, for there was good temper in the mouth, and a cheery brightness in the eyes, which more than a fair share of sensitive pride and unwillingness to brook control had hitherto failed to mar.

'Madonna Santissima! Then you still linger here?'

Startled from his reverie by the masculine voice at his elbow, and the touch of a hand upon his arm, Connisterre wheeled quickly round. Immediately the absent expression upon his face changed to a smile of welcome —a smile which displayed a row of white even teeth and lay like a ray of sunshine over every feature.

'Why, yes,' he said, turning back again to pick up his letters, while the officer by whom he had been accosted looked interestedly on, a cigar between his teeth. 'I arranged to leave this morning but was stopped at the last moment. I am off to Rome to-morrow.'

'Corpo di Bacco! that is as Fate wills,' said the Italian, carelessly flicking the ash from his cigar.

Connisterre surveyed his letters with some eagerness. One addressed in a pretty feminine hand bore the Roman post-mark ; this he conveyed to his pocket with a sudden accession of colour deepening his sunburn ; the second, a card, dated from England, he read over as he stood there, and the third—well, at the third he scarcely glanced, being occupied with parrying the raillery of his companion, whose quick mischievous eyes had noted both the feminine writing upon the first letter and Connisterre's embarrassment.

'So sets the wind, *amico mio*,' he said, linking his arm with easy familiarity in the Englishman's, as they moved away together. 'While the earth revolves upon its axis, while the blue sky smiles down upon this gay world of ours, so long shall the God of Love have dominion over us poor weak men. Sapristi! were it not that the Fates are merciful, I myself should ere now have fallen a victim to the toils of the little wicked one, but the devil take us all! I am cast in a different mould; the toys and playthings of the hour make no lasting impression upon me, for, see you, a beautiful woman is plain to-morrow; eyes which charmed you last night in the whirl of the waltz, or under the stars in our soft beguiling southern heat, have lost their glamour this morning; the flower which fell from her bosom, and which you pressed perchance a moment to your lips, is faded even as her memory——.' Bernini made a slight graceful gesture with his fingers, was silent a moment, then went on more quickly, an ironical vein of humour underlying the liquid Italian voice.

'But you—you are different. Tell me, what is the charm in your cold northern women which holds you constant for a week, a month, a year, possibly even a lifetime, when the brightness of her eyes has faded, when her face has lost its roundness, and her dainty figure spoiled by the cares of matron-hood, its graceful curves; are they more beautiful than ours, more loving, more tender, more seductive? I admire your English women—but explain it to me.'

'It is impossible to explain,' said Connisterre, rather coldly. A slight frown had come over his face; some quick lines of that same demon of pride made themselves apparent about his mouth. He gave a little impatient movement, as if he would fain have shaken off the touch of his companion's arm, but the signs of disquiet or annoyance vanished ere they had sprung fairly into birth, and the light-hearted young Italian rattled on again.

'Of your women I know little, signore,' he pursued, casting a devil-me-care, rollicking glance over his shoulder at a knot of English girls discussing Italian millinery and Italian fashions before the window of an adjacent shop. 'For see you now, it is not easy to make acquaintance with your countrywomen, who attract and repel, encourage and condemn, ere my watch has time to count

the space of one half minute. They will
favour me, especially the young ones, with a
glance of interest, admiration, encourage-
ment in their dancing eyes. I am of all
things a gallant. I would be ashamed to
omit returning that glance, and if per Dio—
how can I help it! for the heart is more
inflammable under the military coat than the
plain civilian dress—if, as I say, the glance
which passes back again to her is warmer in
its ardour, if deeming myself half invited, I
retrace my steps to render further homage,
why then, I am repulsed at once; eyes which
a moment before smiled at me in coquetry
are turned away in scorn, lips which I would
have sworn were full of laughter are now
curved in disdain; even my southern warmth
is not proof against it. I shiver, I tremble,
and as it were shape myself into a glacier.
Talk not to me of English women, Signore
Connisterre. If they would not encourage,
they should not glance; if they would remain
unnoticed, they should cease to take notice.'

Feeling himself at a disadvantage, and conscious of a great deal of lurking truth in the wily Italian's words, Connisterre returned no answer. They had now reached the piazza, and paused as if by mutual consent at the entrance to the Merceria.

'You are going—where?' asked Bernini, with childish readiness to accommodate himself to his companion's plans. 'For myself I have nothing on hand save a coffee with some of our's at Florian's which may well give way to my inclination to see more of you, since to-morrow we must say *addio*. I have found so much pleasure in your society, signore, I would gladly avail myself of it until the latest moment. That is,' courteously, 'if by doing so I shall not render myself tiresome, or what you call in English a "spoil sport."'

'Oh no, certainly not; I have no sport on hand,' returned Connisterre, with a laugh. 'Suppose we take a gondola to the Gardens and return by the quay to my hotel. I shall be glad if you can dine there with me, and afterwards we may strike a little amusement; some music, perhaps, somewhere. We have plenty of time before dinner,' he added, looking at his watch.

To this Bernini gladly assented, and Connisterre, nothing loth to have company on this last evening, which had threatened to hang a little heavily upon his hands, felt grateful to the chance which had wafted the gay Italian in his path. True, there was that about Carlo Bernini, as about most of these young, shallow-pated officers, something which jarred upon him—a vein of loose morality, a careless handling of subjects which Connisterre, like most respectable Englishmen, deemed sacred; but Bernini was a good fellow enough at heart, neither better nor worse than the generality of his class, extravagant perhaps, but generous withal, and possessing traits of courage, daring, candour, and affection, as might in happier circumstances, untainted by the hot blood and dominant passions of the race which had given him birth, have produced a noble character. He amused Connisterre, even interested him, for the young Italian's vanity, his arrogant opinion of the perfection of his own looks, position, race, and family, his innocent, unassumed surprise if any one doubted it, were an enjoyable study in themselves. There is no doubt the complex character of the Italian has much in it to fascinate an Englishman, possessing as it does every characteristic different to his own. The heart of a child, the vanity of a savage, coupled with such quick generosity, strong affections, intense curiosity, gratitude for favours past and present, all mingle so inconsistently with deep-seated treachery, a readiness to take offence even to bloodshed, that it must ever remain an unfathomable problem to the colder-natured, more undemonstrative northerner, as a something which he cannot hope to understand.

CHAPTER II

THE LETTER

Pray do not jest ! This is no time for it.
SHAKESPEARE.

THE heat of the day had waned a little, and a slight breeze, gentle as that of a zephyr's wing, just stirred the placid waters of the lagoon into baby ripples, when Connisterre and his companion stepped into one of the waiting gondolas and gave themselves up to the full enjoyment of an exquisite afternoon in May. For a while no sound, save the rhythmical splashing of the gondolier's oar and the lapping of the waters under the boat's prow broke the perfect stillness. Bernini had sunk into a reverie, and the Englishman, taking advantage of his companion's abstraction, was profiting by it to study the letters he had lately received.

That the one bearing the Roman post-mark was not altogether to his satisfaction might be judged from a slight frown which contracted his even brows, and a restless twitching at his moustache with one sunburnt hand ; but his face cleared at last, and replacing the note, for its length scarcely justified the appellation of a letter, within his pocket, he drew out a second, raising his eyes a moment to glance towards a passing steamer plying its way to the Lido with a flutter and a dash which in themselves seemed a tacit insult to the dignified waters of the Adriatic, and the silent, once powerful city whose base it washed. Bernini roused himself and muttered an Italian imprecation ; the steamer shot swiftly past, all was quietness again. Connisterre turned his attention to the letter which he held in his hand, and surveyed its address with lazy curiosity.

Signore G. Connisterre,
Poste Restante,
Venezia.

The writing, unfamiliar to Geoffrey, was careless, even untidy, running off here and there
into unauthorised curves and twists, with a
curious tremor underlying all, as if the hand
which had penned the lines trembled from
bodily weakness or mental agitation. It bore
the stamp of the little Principality of Monaco,
dated three days before. Connisterre's negligence in not applying for his letters earlier
had caused the delay in receipt, and trusting
the contents were of no importance, he tore
the letter open. It was short, concise, and
puzzled him.

HOTEL DE LA TORRE, MONTE CARLO.

Dear Boy—Let bygones be bygones, and come to
me at once. I am dying in this cursed hole.—Yours,

R. DEANE.

In some bewilderment, Geoffrey read and re-
read the scribbled note which contained such
an imperative summons. Deane? Deane?
The only man he knew of that name had
formerly been a college friend of his own at
Merton, rusticated in his second term for

inveterate gambling and worse, but for whom he had always entertained a warm liking. How this same Deane came to know of his present sojourn in Venice, Connisterre could only conjecture, until he suddenly recollected that a few days earlier he had come across an acquaintance in the Academie Belle Arti, who had been recently in the unfortunate Deane's society, and was intending to join him later on at Nice. He it was who had probably told Deane of Connisterre's where-abouts.

Unpleasant and inconvenient though the request might be, nobody could for one moment dream of ignoring it. The claims of friendship and humanity demanded instant fulfilment of the dying man's wish, but Geoffrey was human enough to grumble a little at this awkward turn of affairs.

'It seems to me that I no sooner over-throw one obstacle which prevents my departure for Rome than another arises,' he said, turning to Bernini, and moodily drag-

ging his fingers through the water. 'I must
be off to Monte Carlo to-night.'

'Monte Carlo! But the season is nearly
over,' said Bernini, in some surprise. 'Leave
your luck to another year, *amico mio*, and
pay your court now to that fair shrine in
Rome. By my soul, signore, were I your
inamorata I should deem it something less
than a compliment if you fled from my
embraces to squander gold at the gaming
tables of that hell on earth, the Casino.'

'It is no gambling fever which lures me
there, I promise you,' broke in Connisterre,
with some heat. 'A deathbed call and the
whirr of the roulette ball have little in common. Drop your jesting, Bernini.'

'A thousand pardons,' exclaimed the
Italian, checking his gay badinage instantly,
but at Connisterre's tone the haughty blood
mounted to his olive-tinted cheeks. 'You
can scarcely blame if I failed to guess the
grave contents of a letter, and passed instead
a senseless gibe at what seemed to me reluct-

ance to join your fair one. If this is not a
sufficient apology, why, indeed, it only re-
quires that——'

But Connisterre, whose knowledge of
Italian character and Italian temper was of
no elementary nature, interrupted him hurriedly, laying his hand in a friendly manner
upon Bernini's arm.

'You are right and I am wrong,' he said,
with an honest laugh. 'I spoke in momentary irritation, annoyed by the upset in my
plans ; let it pass.'

Bernini's brow cleared as if by magic.
He inquired interestedly the particulars of
the news which had so seriously discomposed
his friend.

'It is a thousand pities I did not call for
my letters earlier,' said Connisterre, tugging
at his moustache, as he re-read the note for
the tenth time. 'The poor devil may be
dead and buried now, but I suppose I must go.'

'And at what time may you start ?'

'That I must find out. I rather fancy

there is a train leaving Venice at 11.15 to-
night for Verona and Milan, or I might go
the other route by Bologna. If I am lucky,
I daresay I shall get on to Monte Carlo
by to-morrow evening, travelling straight
through, of course. It is the deuce of a
nuisance though.'

'So it is,' agreed Bernini sympathetically,
and then he launched off into some rollicking
story of his own experiences at Monte Carlo,
which lasted until they were put ashore at the
gardens. It was quiet and peaceful enough
there, deserted, save for a few children playing by the beds of white and purple iris, and
a couple of artisans who lay asleep on one of
the rustic benches, their curly black hair and
swarthy olive-hued faces forming a picture
which only the brush of a Murillo could have
conveyed to canvas.

Connisterre and his companion strolled
leisurely along past the gorgeous beds of
roses and geranium, the dusky alleys thick
with trees, and the groups of laughing chil-

dren, until they found themselves in a long avenue lined on either side with acacia trees in full bloom, the soft white petals from which, stirred by a gentle breeze, floated down like a shower of fairy scented snow, and lay in frothy heaps on the gravelled road.

'Italy, Italy, land of sunshine and of flowers, what artist could ever hope to do you justice!' exclaimed Connisterre, drawing a long breath, as his beauty-loving eyes drank in every detail of the fair picture before them. 'Sometimes I am almost tempted to lay aside the brush for ever, Bernini, and take to hewing stones by the roadside. One's best efforts come so far, so lamentably far short of one's ideal. Imagine trying to convey this,' sweeping his hand towards the flowering acacias and the brilliant peeps of the blue Adriatic at his left, 'to canvas. Bah! it is an impossibility, a dream, Come, let us be going. It is late.'

They turned then, and leaving the avenue behind, walked more quickly on through a rambling, rather dirty street, which led them finally over numerous bridges to the quay, at the further end of which lay the Hotel d'Angleterre, where Connisterre was staying, Carlo Bernini, whose spirits had been inordinately high for the last half hour, sobered down a little as they came in sight of the quay, and beyond exchanging some humorous salutations with his brother officers, behaved for him in a wonderfully rational manner ; but his eyes were roving hither and thither, resting now and then in insolent admiration upon some fair-featured girl, whose suddenly crimsoned cheek, half-fleeting smile, or haughty look, testified to the discomposing glance of his bold dark eyes. Connisterre, who found this kind of thing intensely objectionable, was moved to comment upon the Italian's behaviour in terms which policy alone ordained should have more raillery than rebuke in them, but Bernini cut his remonstrances short with an easy contemptuous laugh.

'To every dog his own collar,' he said

carelessly. 'If it suits you to wear it tight, why grumble that choice leads me to select one with more freedom of breath? You respect the sex; I admire, but scarcely revere it. Who shall say whether it is most my fault or theirs that I hold the name of woman lightly, or think they receive my attentions with less pleasure than I offer them? It is a question which I have neither interest nor energy to solve, so we will leave it in abeyance,' and casting the subject of conversation as lightly aside as the ash from his half-consumed cigar, Bernini plunged into a string of military anecdotes which lasted until they were fairly within the doors of the Hotel d'Angleterre.

CHAPTER III

He carries anger as the flint bears fire.—SHAKESPEARE.

THE hotel guests had all assembled, and the fish was quickly following upon the first course, when the two young men reappeared, and passing through the first room, which opened into a second and larger one, sat down almost at the end of a long table which formed three sides of a square, giving the guests on one side a comprehensive view of the quay outside, from which a faint clatter of steps, the rippling sound of the steamers puffing through the waters of the grand canal, and a modulated hum of voices floated softly in through the open windows.

Opposite to Connisterre were two ladies, evidently mother and daughter, whose fashionable attire, curled and frisetted hair and youthful demeanour, were all called in aid to defy the ravages which time had made upon complexions florid probably in their best days, and figures whose pronounced *embonpoint* was only kept in check by the style of the costumier. The attention of the elder lady, and indeed that of her daughter also, was riveted upon a dignitary of the Church, whose position at the extreme end of the table enabled him to survey the whole company, and sweep a glance of—one might almost say—clerical insolence over the faces around him. This gentleman was in a harsh, dictatorial voice, advancing his opinion with reference to some subject upon which doubtless he considered himself the only competent authority present.

'Oh thank you, thank you so much, for the explanation,' exclaimed Connisterre's *vis-à-vis*, as the divine concluded his remarks; 'you always explain things in so very clear and comprehensible a manner that it perhaps tempts one to trespass unduly upon your kindness!'

'Not at all, not at all,' he returned, with a wave of the right hand, thereby displaying a massive signet-ring which adorned his little finger. 'It is a great pleasure to have so intelligent an auditor.'

While this little interchange of compliments was taking place, Bernini had found amusement in watching the antics of a pinch-faced, shrewish-looking woman opposite to him, whose persistent polishing of her forks, spoons, and glass with a serviette before commencing her dinner, conveyed very little compliment to the waiters. Having finished this to her satisfaction, she craned her head round to stare disapprovingly at two very daintily dressed young girls, who were sitting some distance away conversing with an American gentleman, a recent arrival, and then turned back again to snap out a curt 'no' to one of the waiters who requested her pleasure with reference to the wine carte.

Meanwhile, the clergyman and his fair left-hand neighbour continued their discourse with such interludes from the elder lady as 'Do you; but of course you will;' or, 'As I remarked to my daughter this afternoon, we will ask Mr. Golightly if that would be our best plan;' or, 'You will be able to set us right about——' etc. This garnishing of the conversation by subtle flattery and scarcely veiled admiration, might well have tickled the self-love of any one less vain than the divine, who apparently revelled in it. There was a lull in the conversation at last while the elder lady, to whom the comfort of others was of small account when compared with her own, requested the head waiter to lower the lights, asserting that the heat was insupportable.

'I am sorry, madame, but if I do so it will perhaps be inconvenient to others,' he returned respectfully, smothering a sharp retort which had arisen to his lips, for this lady had been a *bête noire* to all the waiters over since her arrival.

'Then open the windows,' she said with asperity. 'I will not submit to be stifled.'

The windows, four in number, French in shape, were, with the exception of the one beside her, already open, and after a momentary hesitation the man stepped forward and opened one-half of this.

'No, not that side, the other,' she said sharply, and then having had the window so arranged that she could feel the benefit of the air, and the other guests, who had not desired it open, the full benefit of the draught, she resumed her conversation with the clergyman.

This gentleman, whose attention had been attracted to Bernini, then carrying on a low-toned discussion in Italian with Connisterre, commenced to vilify Italians, and especially Italian officers, in no measured terms, trusting perhaps, as so many of us are so apt to do, in the inability of the foreigner to understand another language but his own. At first Bernini, who knew sufficient English to follow the conversation, paid no attention, until suddenly a chance word, uttered rather more loudly than the rest, caught his ear; he turned at once, flashing a look upon the clergyman which might well have warned him off dangerous ground; but Mr. Golightly, oblivious to the gathering storm, proceeded undeterred:

'As I was saying, although for pleasure, instruction, or health, we come into this abandoned land, there is every reason why we should avoid too close intercourse with the Italians themselves, who have from time immemorial been addicted to vices of lying, deceit, and treachery. You agree with me, I am sure,' he added, turning to his right-hand neighbour, a benevolent looking old clergyman, who submitted to the patronage of his reverend brother, possibly because he deemed it beneath his dignity to resent it.

'Far from that,' he replied, speaking with some gravity. 'I have yet to learn, sir, that they are worse than other men, neither do

I consider it consistent with our justice, as Englishmen, to revile so many faults in them, when we, as a nation, have a corresponding number of our own for which to answer.'

'Such may be your opinion, but it is not mine,' retorted the other, roused now to a show of anger by the very calmness of the rebuke. 'Take their army officers, for instance, whose very attentions to an Englishwoman are an insult rather than a compliment. Profligate, treacherous, dishonourable——'

'Gran Dio!' thundered Bernini, starting to his feet, with an imprecation which arrested the attention of every one in his vicinity. 'I would have you know, signore, that I, as an Italian officer and a gentleman, will not suffer you thus to insult my country and her people with your vile and cowardly calumnies, and I would have you know also that were it not we never war with priests or women, I would spill your blood with as little compunction as I fling this wine in your face.' Bernini, as he spoke, placed his hand upon his glass, and crimson to the temples, half-choking with rage, discharged its contents full in the face of the astonished clergyman. There was instant confusion, an outcry of voices, one or two ladies screamed, and for a moment it seemed as if some disgraceful uproar would ensue ; but Bernini, flinging his card upon the table, brought the affair to a summary close by marching out of the room, his dark, passionate eyes sweeping the faces of the startled diners with angry defiance and contempt.

'And *you*, sir, do you think it to your credit as an Englishman to suffer an Italian *roué* to thus insult a countryman in your presence,' shouted Mr. Golightly, wiping the steaming wine from his face, as Connisterre rose to follow his friend.

'I think it as much to mine, as such a display of insolent and contemptible prejudice is to yours,' retorted Geoffrey, who, if he had an Englishman's natural distaste for a scene, yet had all an Englishman's indignation that a guest of his should receive an insult at the table to which he had bidden him. ' May I recommend you, for the future, to abstain from slanderous statements, and cultivate such graces of charity and consideration as are, I believe, enjoined upon gentlemen of your cloth.' He waited an instant, giving his adversary time to reply, but receiving no answer, continued more courteously—' On behalf of my friend, who, in cooler moments will regret, equally with myself, that any action of his should seem to imply a disregard for the presence of ladies, you will perhaps allow me to apologise.' Then with a bow to the ladies in his vicinity, Connisterre also left the table.

CHAPTER IV

EN ROUTE FOR MONACO

It grieves me much to see this quarrel between gentlemen.
                                            Spanish Student.

PASSING quickly down the long room between
the rows of astonished, amused, or indignant
guests, the bewildered waiters, and incensed
authorities of the hotel, who, hearing the
sudden uproar and hum of voices, had hurried
to the spot, Connisterre made his way outside
to the quay, and looked about with some
anxiety for the hot-tempered Italian. Fortu-
nately, only a few seconds had elapsed since
he disappeared, and after a little difficulty the
Englishman's search was rewarded. He came
up with Bernini just as the latter was descend-
ing the steps to one of the waiting gondolas.
Carlo turned fiercely round. He had flung

on the short blue cloak common to the officers, and faced Connisterre muffled in its protecting folds, one corner thrown over his left shoulder screening his features from view.

' I think I have scarcely merited such curt treatment at your hands,' said Geoffrey, speaking very quietly. ' Much as I regret this unfortunate fracas and the insult which you have received, yet, since personally I am quite blameless in the matter, it is hardly courteous, signore, to leave so hastily, giving me no opportunity to express my regret, nor say farewell.'

The even temperate words were not without their effect, even upon the hot-tempered Italian. In a half apologetic voice he murmured his regrets for the haste which Connisterre had been obliged to make in following him, but even as he spoke other and darker thoughts were at work within his mind, and it needed but little skill to divine their tenor, even before he broke out into a torrent of vituperative wrath against his late antagonist.

Connisterre listened in silence, and after a time Bernini cooled down, checking his words with a contemptuous laugh.

'Why do I waste my breath! You are an Englishman, you do not understand. You deem this unnecessary vehemence, bad form, execrable taste, and everything else by which your nation, too phlegmatic to take fire, crushes itself into the similitude of a log. I will say no more.'

'Listen, Signore Bernini,' replied Connisterre, smothering an angry retort; 'let us be candid. I admit you have been almost unbearably insulted; I admit your right to resent it; but surely a moment's calm reflection should show you that you are unjust. If my countryman has uttered words to annoy you, think whether your hasty commentary upon the faults and failings of my nation may not be equally annoying to me. I have not actually resented your raillery,—let us term it that for want of a better word,—or endeavoured upon the strength of it to pick a quarrel with you, not that I am by any means less prone to see the sarcasm, but because I am fully assured neither you nor I can form a just estimate of the other's faults, and I ask you whether, personally, I have done any-thing to merit your forcing this man's quarrel upon my shoulders?'

'You say that you have cause to resent my words,' exclaimed Bernini, dropping the corner of his cloak and revealing a face full of hate and passion. 'I am willing to give you satisfaction. Will you fight?'

'No,' said Connisterre, steadily; 'I am neither anxious to lose my life nor take yours. The day has gone by when men, to wipe away a fancied smear upon their honour, stained their hands in each other's blood. I am not deficient in courage, signore, but I will not fight you. Come,' he added, after a short pause, speaking in a friendly voice, 'my pride as a gentleman and self-respect as a man forbid me to say more. Will you not part as friends? I am heartily sorry this should have occurred.'

It would have taken some one far more churlish and resentful than Carlo Bernini to resist the charm of Connisterre's face and manner, the honest, steady look in his eyes, the genuine cordiality in his voice.

'No, no, you are right,' he exclaimed impulsively, gripping Geoffrey's hand; 'we will indeed be friends.'

'And you will forget the insult you have received?' went on Connisterre, mindful perhaps of the dark side of Italian nature.

'Since you wish it, yes; but he has only your intercession to thank that he does not receive three inches of cold steel in his body to-night. Ah, you look, you are surprised! but we Italians are too proud to take an injury to court for a gilded salve. It is better to silence a slanderous tongue than bind it temporarily with law cords. But you need not fear for his tender skin, he is quite

safe, so long as he does not cross my path
again with his vile words and viler insinua-
tions.'

Convinced by the sincerity of Bernini's
manner that there was no further risk of
deadly consequences to the evening's dis-
agreement, Connisterre turned the subject of
the conversation to his own immediate departure, and after a little hesitation Carlo
agreed to return with him to the hotel.
Connisterre had still his portmanteau to pack
and other arrangements to make, which would
take up all the intervening time before his
train left Venice.

When an hour later the two men em-
barked in a gondola for the station, the
beauty and intoxication of a Venetian night
were at their height. Silently, sheer out of
the water as it seemed, rose stately palaces,
where once had dwelt all the pride and
beauty of Venetian nobility, and which
reveal even now, in their defaced fronts and
time-stained walls, a restful dignity they

will never wholly lose. Years may come
and go, Empires rise and fall, dynasties
change and democracy add day by day to its
swelling tide, but neither time nor the hand
of man can take away while one stone stands
upon another in that silent city, her luring
beauty, intoxicating charm, and strange im-
perious fascination, which defies the pen of
the poet or the brush of the artist to describe.
Something of this was perhaps passing
through the mind of Geoffrey Connisterre as
he sat silently gazing out into the darkness of
the grand canal. Here and there the gondolas of the singers, bright with coloured
lanterns, and gay with cheery voices singing
out in a wild refrain, made a brilliant spot in
the gloomy shadows, or the steel-prowed,
griffin-headed gondolas clustered together in
a dark phalanx, broke up suddenly, moving
in and out, sending a flash of light glittering
from their prows across the darkness as they
crept up in ghostly silence side by side.
Then as the gondola shot forward on its way

the coloured lights of the Chinese lanterns
faded into evanescent golden balls, the voices
of the minstrels grew faint,—faint but inex-
pressibly sweet, until at last all was silence,
save the lapping of the water, and the
hoarse 'Stali, stali' of the gondolier as
he turned to thread his craft through the
grim tortuous side canals which intersect
the city.

Connisterre roused from his reverie as
they neared the steps leading to the quay
before the station, and after a liberal douceur
to the boatmen walked on with his companion
into the midst of the roar and confusion consequent upon the departure of the Verona
train.

How little he guessed in the midst of his
conversation with Bernini, that the threads
of an adverse fate were even then imper-
ceptibly drawing him further and further
away from the old calm life to the unknown
world before him ; how little he dreamed of all
that was to come and go before he again

stood upon the platform of the Venice station. And yet, even despite his absorption in the present, he was conscious of an odd moment- ary change in himself, an indefinable instinct which impelled him to pause in the middle of a jest with Bernini, and turn an interested gaze towards a young man at that moment placing his portmanteau upon a truck before them. There was nothing in the careless, unmistakably English face, with its blue eyes and drooping fair moustache to call even for a second glance, but to Connisterre it seemed strangely familiar, as if there lay between them an impalpable link of something un- known, something which was yet to have its influence upon the lives of both himself and this stranger.

The presentiment lasted but a moment; with an inward smile at his own childishness, Connisterre resumed his conversation at the precise place where he had broken off, the stranger moved aside with a 'pardon mon- sieur' for inadvertently stopping the way, and the wheels of destiny forced them again apart, but the clue to all the labyrinth of doubt and perplexity which was henceforth to become part of Geoffrey Connisterre's life, lay in the stranger's hands.

CHAPTER V

A MISTAKEN IDENTITY

Men should be what they seem.—SHAKESPEARE.

IT was late in the afternoon of the following
day when Connisterre reached the end of his
wearisome journey, and emerged into the
light and gaiety of the garden of the
Riviera, Monte Carlo. High above him the
Casino, a blaze of white and gold and blue,
glittered in the powerful rays of a sun which
penetrated every corner, flooding the flowers
and terraced walks, the blooming myrtle
hedges, the palms and giant olives, the
climbing roses, and the delicate lavender-
tinted westeria with a wonderful glory.
Connisterre, tired with incessant travelling,
thirsty, hot, and half-choked with dust,

heaved a little sigh of relief when he had jumped into one of the waiting fiacres, and was driving to Deane's hotel.

A light, soft breeze, indescribably fragrant, filled with the odours of a thousand flowers, blew refreshingly across his temples, and he bared his head to meet it, his beauty-loving eyes drinking in the fairness of the scene before him. He would be indeed a churl who could gaze upon Monte Carlo without one quickening pulse or thrill of admiration, or fail to appreciate that peep of Monaco out there which stands out against the blue background of sky, guiltless alike of cloud or darkness, that inimitable stretch of azure water, washing its snowy base, or curling back in foam-clad wavelets over the jutting rocks. Here nature has laid on her choicest colours, decked it with the · treasures of a myriad flowers, given alike the grateful shade of tree-lined dusky paths and brilliant sunshine, and wrapped the blue sea, like the mantle of some dainty woman, about its shoulders. A

paradise, truly paradise, such as the eyes of
our first parents may have gazed upon in the
birthday of the world; but a paradise cor-
rupted now into a hell, by reason of its
crimes and wickedness, and the foot of sinful
man. Despite its beauty, its flowers, and
sunshine, it reeks with infamy from every
pore; wickedness cries aloud from the garish
walls of the Casino, vice stalks rampant
through the corridors, despair hides its shame-
covered head beneath the myrtle - covered
paths, while at its heart a canker eats through
the fairest rind, and reveals the hideous decay
within.

When Connisterre reached the hotel and
jumped out of the fiacre he paused a moment,
looking towards a little group of people
loitering upon the steps before the door.
The usual group; he was no stranger to it.
A handsome foreign woman, dressed in the
height of fashion, who surveyed him boldly
through her *pince nez;* an effeminate, puling
youth, with an incipient moustache, and vice

written in every lineament; a tall, slender
man, with a dissipated look and evil gray
eyes; an older one, carefully dressed, trim
and dapper, with a parchment-like skin and
beady eyes. Two apparently very bored
American girls standing apart from the
others; an Englishman reading his paper
with the unemotional air peculiar to the
British tourist abroad; a couple of elderly,
play-infected old women—a group such as he
had witnessed times out of number during
his frequent visits to Monte Carlo. He
walked on into the hotel, which felt refreshingly cool after the glare outside.

'I wish to see M. Deane,' he said in
French to one of the waiters. 'I understand
that he is staying here;' then, as the man
instead of replying only darted a curious
glance at him, he repeated the request in
Italian.

'Pardon, monsieur, je parle français,' said
the waiter hurriedly. 'Monsieur Deane il
est——' But at that moment a gentlemanly-

looking man, who had overheard the alter-
cation, came up to them, and the waiter went
forward with the rest to meet the hotel
omnibus which had clattered up to the door
and was discharging its freight of passengers
and luggage.

'You wish to see Monsieur Deane?' said
the new-comer civilly ; but he cast a careful
glance around him, and drew Geoffrey into a
small room, an office apparently, before he
spoke again.

'I very much regret to inform you that
Mr. Deane died this morning,' he said in a
low voice. 'Pardon, monsieur, I beg of you
to remember we may be overheard'—this
with an accent of keen annoyance, as Geoffrey,
startled by the information, repeated the word
'dead,' and fell back a step.

'Then I am too late?'

'Too late by some hours. Monsieur
Deane, I think, expected you yesterday.
He died quite suddenly about eleven this
morning, and the body has been removed

to the mortuary.   It will be interred early
to-morrow morning.

'And the cause of death?'

'A chill and some long standing heart
affection.   Madame will be relieved by your
arrival.'

'He was not alone, then—M. Deane?'
asked Connisterre, turning to leave the room.

'Alone?' said the other in some surprise.
'Oh no, monsieur; madame was with him
to the last.   She is in very great grief.
Angelo'—this to one of the waiters—'show
this gentleman, Monsieur Connisterre, to
No. 37.   You will find madame there,' he
added to Geoffrey.

'Madame,' repeated Connisterre under
his breath.   'The plot deepens.'   His reflections as he followed the waiter up a succession
of stairs and along numerous corridors were
not of the pleasantest.   His natural instincts
warred against the idea of being mixed up in
anything discreditable, and knowing that the
ill-fated Deane possessed neither mother,

sister, nor wife, who could have been with him at this juncture ; the probabilities pointed to some relationship which the world would be ready to disclaim. However, having come so far, the young man did not feel disposed to turn back now at the eleventh hour.

' I must go through with it,' he murmured, when they paused before No. 37, and the waiter knocked softly. There was no response, but a second summons elicited a faint reply in a girlish voice.

' Entrez.'

' C'est monsieur votre mari, madame,' said the waiter opening the door, and he stepped aside to permit of Connisterre following him ; ' Monsieur Connisterre.'

As he uttered the words, a girl, the only occupant of the small room, who was crouching, huddled up on a couch near the window, jumped to her feet with a cry like that of some child which sees in its distress and loneliness the familiar face of one bringing protection with his presence, and before

Connisterre could recollect himself or explain away the mistake, had flung herself into his arms in a passion of hysterical weeping.

'Oh, it is you, it is you!' she exclaimed in French, between her sobs. 'Why did you not come sooner? he is dead, Gerard, dead.'

Then the waiter went softly out, closing the door behind him.

CHAPTER VI

THE PLOT THICKENS

I am just going to leap into the dark.—RABELAIS.

CONNISTERRE, thus taken by surprise, astounded, overwhelmed, confused by the clinging arms and tear-stained cheek pressed against his own, remained for a few moments the passive recipient of caresses which a sense of tingling shame told him were his only by some hideous mistake; but almost immediately his self-possession returned, and with it a friendly wish to do what he could to help the girl in her grief.

'Pardon, mademoiselle, I—I am truly sorry,' he said, releasing her arms but retaining one little hand in kindly clasp; 'there must be some mistake. I do not think we——'

At the sound of that deep musical voice,
the girl, hardly as she seemed at first sight
more than a child, flung away his detain-
ing hand and retreated to the farther end of
the room, gazing at him with amazement
and distress in her big dark eyes. She was
a slim, pale little thing, with a piquante
foreign face, disfigured by tears lately shed
and the heavy grief pressing upon her. In
the crimsoned eyelids, the weary drop of
the lips, Connisterre read signs of a lonely
vigil, the long days and nights spent by a
dying bed, the awful despair which the end
had brought upon her, and his own distress
at having increased her perplexities by his
advent there grew deeper.

'But you—you are not Gerard,' she gasped.
'You have his face, his eyes, but not his
voice. You are like him, but—— Oh,
what shall I do, what shall I do?' She
broke off, wringing her hands and shrinking
away from him like a frightened child as he
approached.

'I confess I do not understand it at all,' he said, fumbling in his pocket for the letter which had been the innocent cause of all the embarrassment. 'I received this from Roger Deane only yesterday. I regret that my negligence in failing to apply for letters at the post office in Venice has resulted in my being unable to see my old friend before he died, but I do trust now that I am here you will allow me to be of some use. I assure you it will be a great pleasure to me if I can help you in any way.'

Insensibly as he spoke the girl had regained some measure of self-control, and although the tears were still chasing one another down her cheeks, she made a visible effort to recover herself, putting out an unsteady hand for the letter which he held towards her.

'I do not know how this came into your possession,' she said in a stifled voice, looking down at the superscription. 'It was written to my husband, Gerard Connisterre, by my father some days ago, asking him to come to us at once. We expected him all yesterday, and I—I thought it was Gerard when you arrived.' Her tears commenced to fall afresh as she spoke. Geoffrey gazed at her in honest bewilderment ; he could not believe his ears had heard aright.

'You cannot be Roger Deane's *daughter*,' he exclaimed desperately. 'Deane! why, he was a younger man than myself.'

'My father's name was Richard, not Roger,' she corrected, striving to check her tears. 'I don't understand why you are here.'

Connisterre pulled his moustache in much perturbation of spirit. There was only one solution to the mystery, and that seemed almost incredible. If, as her words seemed to imply, there was another Connisterre in Venice, then he, Geoffrey, had unwittingly purloined this man's letters. Something not unlike a curse upon the *Poste Restante* system rose to his lips. This other Connisterre, then, who was he? The name was an uncommon one, he could count his relatives upon the fingers of one hand, and knew also that personally he could not by any chance be mistaken for one of them. That there must be some striking resemblance between this other man, whose letters he had appropriated, and himself, the girl's reception of him had testified. It would be impossible to conceive a more embarrassing sequence of events. To have introduced himself un-requested into the heart of a domestic drama, to have passed even for a moment amongst a crowd of waiters and under the eyes of the hotel proprietor himself as this girl's husband, to have passively received her endearments in the presence of a third person, all these harassing reflections crowded thickly upon Connisterre as he stood there deliberating how best to meet them.

'It is most unfortunate,' he exclaimed aloud, with genuine regret both for himself and his distressed companion, whose position every moment was rendered more and more equivocal ; 'there is some misconception here. To be brief, Mrs. Connisterre' (how strange it seemed to call her by his own name), ' I was totally unaware of the existence of another man in Venice bearing my own patronymic, and when I applied for my letters at the *Poste Restante* department yesterday this one from your father was handed to me amongst the rest. The contents puzzled me, but knowing that my friend Roger Deane had lately been staying at Monte Carlo, and also that he was in indifferent health, I concluded the summons came from him, and at once started in response. Will you, if it is not too painful, explain the situation to me, and failing the presence of your husband, allow me to be of some use. I shall, of course, telegraph and write to Venice at once, as it is quite possible that he may again apply for his letters.'

' There is not much to explain,' said the

girl, dropping her eyes in some embarrassment, while the hot colour surged up into
her face. 'I—have not seen my husband
for some time, nearly a year, but my father
knew that he was in Venice, and so wrote to
him to come. He felt that he—was going
to die, and it troubled him to know I should
be alone.'

'Yes,' said Connisterre, encouragingly, as
she paused, overcome by the sad recollections
which swept over her.

'I—I do not think he *will* come,' the girl
burst out suddenly, her tears drying on her
flaming cheeks, her hands nervously clasping
and unclasping. We have quarrelled—at
least—that is he and my father did, and then
Gerard left us. He said he would never see
me again, so we have lived on alone, my
father and I. But I hoped against hope he
would come to me now that I am left alone.
I do not know where I must go, nor what I
ought to do. I have only very little money,
and—and they will not believe here that I

spoke the truth when I said my husband——'
She broke off again in an agony of sobs.

Connisterre, who had seated himself beside
her upon the couch, was full of pity and
compassion. Gently, with infinite tact, he
succeeded, by dint of skilful questioning, in
making out amidst the sobs and tears, the
incoherent words and gestures, that her
father, who had been evidently an habitué
of the gaming tables, had left her, as might
be expected, totally unprovided for, save for
a small sum of ready money, which the
funeral expenses would nearly swallow, and
that the proprietor, who had brought in
a bill of five hundred francs for damages
consequent upon the death, had cast insulting aspersions upon the girl's statement that
her husband would come to the rescue,
hinting, more or less broadly, that madame
might not be able to claim a legal protector.
Connisterre ground his teeth as he listened.
There came into his mind a fragment of a
book he had once read—

'What is it to be a woman, my mother?'

'It is to be a target for the coward world to shoot its arrows at, with the sure and certain conviction that the victim can seek no redress. It is to have the hand of every man against you, to suffer, to submit, to die quietly, when life becomes impossible. That is what sometimes it is to be a woman, bereft of father and brother, my child.'

In a moment Connisterre seemed to realise the awful responsibility which now devolved upon himself. As a man of the world, he saw clearly enough the inference which would be drawn should he openly disclaim the relationship. His appearance there, his reception, witnessed most unfortunately by the waiter, could bear but one interpretation. Either he was this girl's husband or she had lied, and the connection between them was less respectable. He felt himself colour under all his healthy sunburn as he reflected upon the invidious position in which they were both placed. He must act now with regard to the future, neither forgetting his chivalry nor underestimating the serious

results which might possibly follow upon
it.   To boldly defy all consequences and
for the nonce play his part before the world
as her husband seemed, if a daring, at least
almost the only step to take.   There was at
all times in Geoffrey Connisterre a certain
indifference to the consequences of his own
acts, which might spring either from a profound faith in his abilities or a careless,
quixotic bravado.   He was a little prone to
acting first and deliberating after, somewhat
at the mercy of his generous impulses,
seldom considering whether he would or
would not eventually become the sufferer by
indulging them.   In the present circumstances, however, to do Geoffrey justice, he
did bring all his mental energies to bear
upon a solution of the difficulty, and it was
only at the last he was reluctantly obliged
to admit that there seemed but one way, and
this the way that had first sprung into his
mind.   He realised that however plausible a
story he might concoct, testifying to the

truth of the girl's statement that she was
indeed expecting her husband, and that he,
Connisterre, unfortunately bearing the same
name and lineaments, had through some
extraordinary accident become possessed of
the letter of this other man, it would bear
a very improbable colour upon the face, and
sound incredible in the ears of those to whom
the most innocent of circumstances savoured
of evil.   Besides there was the damning
evidence of the girl's reception.   It was possible, of course, to fabricate some story as to
a previous acquaintance with her, to state
that she was his brother's wife; but Connisterre was proud almost to a fault, tenacious of his honour, loathing prevarication in
every form, and he could not bring himself
to the utterance of a deliberate lie.   There
seemed nothing for it but to quietly acquiesce
in the situation, to neither confirm nor deny,
to give her his protection for a few hours,
and then without delay remove her from
Monte Carlo to some temporary home until

the real husband could be found and forced
to take up his responsibilities. Not a very
wise decision to come to, perhaps, but it is
easy to blame and not so easy to advise.
Few even of the wisest of us could have
found a satisfactory path out of this labyrinth
of perplexity save the narrow and rugged
one of truth. This, viewed in every light
that Geoffrey could throw upon it, held some
risk of smirching the girl's white robe of
womanhood. Had it not been for the com-
promising nature of his reception, the young
man would in all probability have boldly
stated the truth, but it seemed impossible
now to explain it away with a hope of receiving credence. He grew bewildered,
uneasy, more and more embarrassed, as he
tried to think the matter over; he could
see but the one way — a mistaken one,
truly—but there was nothing else to be done.

'Mrs. Connisterre,' he said at last, and
the earnestness of his voice caused her to
look up at him with a little start. Their

eyes met, hers tearful and questioning, his very grave and friendly. 'I cannot help inferring from your manner that you think you have cause to fear misconception and annoyance through your husband's absence and my unfortunate arrival. That being so, it devolves upon me as a gentleman to save you from it. This strange coupling of names, this similarity of feature, this story sounds so—so——' He stumbled for a word, slurred it over, then went on more quickly. 'Let the consequences be what they may, I could not put you to the pain of having your word doubted; in short—I am saying it very badly, but what I wish to suggest, you must not hesitate to say if it is displeasing to you—that since it is entirely my fault you are placed in such an unpleasant position, owing I mean to my having appropriated your husband's letter, let me for a time assume all his responsibilities. There is no necessity for us to enter into any explanation to the people here.

The girl's eyes dropped, while a vivid glow of colour crept into her cheek.

'Believe me, it is the only way,' urged Connisterre. 'It will save you all annoyance while you are here, and to-morrow morning we could leave Monte Carlo for some place where your husband will come to you.'

She did not answer; so after a momentary pause, Geoffrey went on again.

'I will write to Venice explaining in full how the mistake has arisen and what steps I have taken to help you. I think he will hold me blameless in the matter, and you can best tell whether there is sufficient resemblance between us to pass current, if later on any of the people who may accidently see me here should meet your husband.'

The girl was playing nervously with the ribbons of her dress, her face was partially averted from him, but he could see the trembling of lip and chin, which told him how greatly she was moved.

'You are very kind,' she said at last in a

low voice. 'But I don't think you quite —understand all. It might mean——'

'I think I do,' he said gently. 'You refer to the monetary part of it, do you not? but, believe me, I am willing—more than willing to offer you substantial help. If you have need of money I will lend it to you. Your husband can repay me at his leisure, or if— if fortune has been unkind to him, and like many others, his good will is deeper than his purse, let us consider the debt cancelled. Our humanity, or Christianity if you like, is worth little if it does not encourage us to hold out a helping hand to those who may require it; besides, I also have known what it is to be hard up—let me by the memory of those days make this time a little smoother for you. Come, Mrs. Connisterre, won't you let me help you?'

'And if my husband should not return— if he has left me for ever, what am I to do then?' she asked, wringing her hands. 'Where am I to go?'

Connisterre was silent. The same idea had occurred to him, but he put it resolutely aside.

'Well,' he said striving to speak with cheerfulness; 'sufficient for the day is the evil thereof. When he knows you are alone he will forget the quarrel and come forward to help you, I am sure. The breach must be a very deadly one which could suffer a man to leave his wife in such a strait as you are now. Have you no friends to whom I can send?'

'Friends!' she laughed a little drearily and walked over to the window, leaning her hand upon the ledge as if for support. 'No, I have no friends—we have led a wandering life always—there is nobody to help me.'

'Yes there is,' said Connisterre, gently. '*I* am going to help you. Poor child, you are not fit to be alone; try to trust me, try to believe I will do what is best for you.' He had followed her to the window and stood looking down upon her with eyes full of compassion. What a child she was, what a helpless lonely bit of a thing to be left to face the world and its pitfalls.

'I have some money,' she said drearily; 'a little, not much; but I think it will be enough to pay for—for to-morrow; then there is the other, too—the five hundred francs—I must pay that, only if I do, I shall have nothing left.'

'You will not pay anything of the kind. I believe that legally he can only claim twenty francs; I will settle that matter for you.'

'But I would rather pay than have any trouble about it,' she said with feverish eagerness. 'I could not, oh! I could not endure it all to be made public.'

'Set your mind quite at rest. There shall be nothing of that kind. Now, will you listen to the remainder of my plan and say if you have anything better to suggest. I ought, of course, to give you some information as to my position, my credentials to respectability and all that ; but it is just a little difficult, and I don't know if you will care to take only my word—it is asking you to trust me to a great extent.'

She looked up at him, a long steady look, Connisterre met it unflinchingly.

'If we were in Rome instead of Monte Carlo everything would be simplified,' he said. 'I have a number of friends there, and could give you plenty of references ; but as we are not, I must ask you to take my word. I am an Englishman as you know, an artist by profession, and can well afford to help you. You must draw upon me if you require more money than you have at present. Now, it seems to me that it would be in every respect better for you to leave here early to-morrow morning and allow me to take you to some friends of mine in Genoa—two old French ladies with whom I have often stayed. They are good, kind-hearted people, and it will be a safe shelter for you while waiting for your husband. If he should have left

Venice we will advertise for him. Do you think you can agree to this arrangement?'

'If you think it is better, yes,' she said with passive submission. 'I cannot stay here. I must trust you.'

Of the enormous faith she was putting in this man, the girl did not realise until long afterwards. She was too young, too childish to fully appreciate the risk.

'You shall not repent it,' said Geoffrey, with steady earnestness. 'Now I want you to promise that you will not trouble about anything further to-night; leave all in my hands. Have you had anything to eat to-day?'

She shook her head, trying in vain to check the tears which would force themselves down her cheeks.

'I will see that you have something sent up at once, and you must eat it. Remember, you have a hard day to-morrow. Is there anything to be arranged about that,' he added in a lower tone.

'No, it is all settled. He is to be buried very early at Mentone.' She shuddered a little as if at some distasteful recollection.

Connisterre glanced towards a clock ticking away on the mantel-shelf. It was later than he had thought.

'Well, I must leave you now,' he said, trying to speak cheerfully. 'Is there anything else I can do for you?' Any one to whom I can write?'

'There is nobody,' she replied. 'I have not any friends at all.' Then she made a little movement towards him, put out her hands blindly and would have fallen to the ground but for Connisterre's outstretched arms.

'At the end of her tether, poor child,' he thought pityingly, as he laid her upon a couch and rang for assistance. 'This is a bad business all through, and I don't think we have seen the end of it yet. Madame has fainted,' he added, turning towards the chambermaid who came into the room at this juncture. 'Fetch some brandy quickly and pass the salts—I think I see some on the table over there. Thank you.'

In a few minutes Léonie Connisterre regained consciousness, and a streak of colour came back into the pale cheeks. She glanced in some bewilderment at Connisterre who was leaning over her and would have risen, but he placed an authoritative hand upon her shoulder, holding a glass of cordial to her lips.

'Drink this before you sit up and then keep very quiet. You were a little faint, that is all. I wish you would take my advice and go to bed. I will see to everything for you.'

'Very well,' she said submissively, evidently too worn out in mind and body to demur. 'You are very good to me, monsieur.' She turned and pressed her lips in an impulsive foreign fashion to the strong hand lying on her shoulder. Connisterre withdrew it and coloured hotly. He was half-touched, half-embarrassed by the action.

'It is nothing,' he said hastily in a low voice. 'I am very glad to be of service to you in any way.' Then he left the room, pausing a moment outside upon the landing to give a few last directions to the chambermaid who had followed him.

'Madame should be kept very quiet; oh yes. She should want for nothing. Monsieur might depend upon her having every comfort and attention.' So said the white-capped, sharp-featured woman, her zeal quickened by the gold coin which Connisterre slipped into her hand. 'Madame was very fatigued by the anxiety of the last few days, but she, Helaire, would take every care of her.'

Circumstances were now beyond Connisterre's control. He had acquiesced in the position. He must abide by it.

CHAPTER VII

A FATAL RECOGNITION

> I am one, my liege,
> Whom the vile blows and buffets of the world
> Have so incensed that I am reckless what
> I do to spite the world.—*Macbeth*, Act iii. Sc. 1.

WITH slow gait and thoughtful brow, Connisterre made his way downstairs, mentally revolving certain plans which reflection alone could render feasible. It was no light responsibility which he had undertaken, and already doubt, that most subtle and harassing enemy to one's peace of mind, was assailing him with her insidious whisperings. Had he in order to save his protégée temporary embarrassment risked a possible scandal? His face grew gloomy as one idea after another crowded disquietingly into his mind. There

were other people to be considered, others
to whom his honour was, or should be dear.
If these learned to doubt him—but pooh,
why face imaginary complications which
might never arise, why trouble himself about
the future when he had only to deal with the
present ; but despite his sophistry, the young
man's hand went involuntarily to the breast
pocket of his coat, where lay that letter with
the Roman post-mark.   If the writer were
to hear some garbled version of this day's
doings, were to even for a moment give
credence to the malicious statement of some
third person, then who could answer for the
consequences ?   Connisterre strangled the
idea ere it well had birth, but the sting
remained, awaiting but the opportunity to
blossom into life.

The fingers of the hall clock were pointing
to half-past six when he reached the foot of
the stairs.   Letters must be written, both
to Genoa and Venice, the hotel proprietor
interviewed, a dozen other matters arranged ;

but as letters were the most important, these should be attended to at once. Geoffrey went off into the library and sat down to write to the other Connisterre in Venice, explaining as fully as he could the urgency of the situation, and enclosing an address where he had determined to remove his charge the following day. Genoa was convenient as a centre, and had this advantage also, that he knew of two old French ladies living there who would willingly take charge of the helpless girl until her husband could be communicated with. His letters finished, Geoffrey went in search of the proprietor, whom he found immersed in correspondence in the office. The interview was a brief one, Connisterre not feeling disposed to waste many words upon the matter. He wished for an account of expenses connected with Mr. Deane's illness, the damages claimed by the hotel on account of death, and all other items for which his daughter was liable.

'My time is very limited, monsieur,' he said, breaking into the elaborate explanation launched forth by Monsieur Delaney as to why his charges had seemed extortionate to madame. 'I am perfectly aware that you *can* make a claim, but I am also aware of the legal extent of that claim. I shall certainly dispute the one you have sent in. Let me have the full account as early as possible; I am willing to reimburse you generously for any inconvenience to which you may have been put, and I think you will see it is to your advantage to meet me; if not, I shall have recourse to the law.' This being what Monsieur Delaney wished to avoid at any cost, he hastily murmured his wishes to settle everything amicably. Ready money was preferable to doubtful litigation, which would be in any case more or less damaging to the hotel. 'He was sure monsieur would be perfectly satisfied with the account.'

'Very well,' said Connisterre, turning

away. 'I think that is all. Will you kindly reserve me a room to-night?'

'And monsieur will dine here?'

'No, I think not.' The inexpediency of dining at the public table had already struck him. He was by no means anxious to run against any familiar face, or be seen more than was avoidable in the hotel. Leaving the office he strolled across the hall and stood a moment at the open door, the letters in his hand. As he did so a gentleman emerged hastily from the smoke room, and catching a glimpse of the tall figure half a dozen yards away, retreated just as hastily, leaving the door a few inches ajar for the purpose of watching Connisterre's movements unobserved.

'Yes it is,' he murmured, leaning forward; 'I thought I could not be mistaken. I wonder what the devil you are doing here while Claudia is waiting for you in Rome, and eating her heart out with mortification and disappointment at your delay. This

is no through route from Venice, *mon
ami.*'

While Connisterre stood there unaware of
the surveillance to which he was being sub-
jected, the head waiter came up to him, but
in spite of his strenuous efforts, the watcher
by the door could only overhear fragments of
the low-toned conversation which ensued.
Something about 'madame,' and 'in her
room,' then an indistinguishable murmur and
'Send it on to Mentone early to-morrow.'
That was all, after which Connisterre went
away. The stranger came out of ambush
and joined the waiter, who was making some
alterations in the case containing the list of
visitor's names.

'Will you tell me the name of that gentleman who has just gone out?' he said, remov-
ing a cigar from his lips. 'His face seems
familiar to me.'

Alphonse looked up, recognising in the
speaker a stranger who had come in to dine
with one of the guests.

'His name? it is Monsieur Connisterre,'
he replied. 'He arrive to-day; he leave the
morning to-morrow.'

'Oh!' The stranger ran his eyes down
the list of names; they paused, staring interestedly at a card near the bottom—

Mrs. G. Connisterre.

'Monsieur Connisterre is not alone then?'
he said, flicking the ash from his cigar.

'Alone? oh no, monsieur; he arrive
alone, but madame she has been here some
time. They will set out to-morrow.'

'Oh, thanks,' drawled the other. 'I
fancied I knew his face. Ah!' he muttered
when the waiter was out of ear-shot, 'this is
what keeps you here, Mr. Geoffrey Connisterre. So much for virtue and constancy,
and all the saintly qualities with which the
vivid imagination of my cousin credits you!
but upon my soul the very flagrancy of the
whole liaison is beyond belief; at least you
might have had the decency to assume another

name, and throw a veil of conventional propriety over your little peccadilloes. You,
you——' he paused as if at a loss for words.
'Well, it is my turn now, I think, Mr. Connisterre—my turn, and it will go hard with me
if I cannot use your frailties to shape my own
ends. Twenty-four hours must see me in
Rome. Ah, Claudia! who is to come between
us now? I know your pride, your sensitive
dignity. They will not stand the strain which
my story will put upon them, and as for your
love, I think it will kill it.'

CHAPTER VIII

OUT OF PITY

> So they sat and played together,
> All the old men and the young men,
> Played for dresses, weapons, wampum,
> Played till midnight, played till morning,
> Played until the Yenadizze,
> Till the cunning Pau-Puk-Keewis,
> Of their treasures had despoiled them.
>
> *The Song of Hiawatha.*

AFTER posting his letters, Geoffrey's next business, and this an important one, was to satisfy the cravings of hunger, which had become unpleasantly arbitrary, and having obtained a fair dinner at one of the other hotels, he went in later on to the Casino, thinking he might pass a couple of hours listening to the music in the theatre. Crowds of people were flocking up the broad flight of steps before the open doorway. Old and young, plain and beautiful, ladies in evening dress, men in concert coats, some passing on into the gambling salons, others through the curtained doorway into the theatre, where the concert had already commenced. Geoffrey followed the latter, and strolling up one of the side aisles, took a seat near the wall, where he had a good view of the whole room. He was tired with the rush and excitement and perplexities of the last few hours, and disinclined for physical effort of any kind. It was restful both to mind and body, sitting there in lazy comfort listening to the intoxicating strains of the Casino band, world-famed for its excellence; interesting to watch the ever-changing audience, the cosmopolitan crowd thronging the gorgeous hall, and to note the varied expressions on the faces of those around him as they drifted in and out, sometimes wandering away to try their luck at the tables, and returning flushed with success or dispirited by failure.

But amongst them all, Geoffrey did not see one familiar face, a fact for which he was profoundly thankful. Softly the music rose and fell, now crashing forth in glorious melody, now sinking into an angel's whisper, which seemed to murmur like an exquisite human voice within the curtained alcoves, or rush out in triumphant song. Then the German love song died into silence, and a wild shriek of Hungarian music rent the air. How it danced, and curveted, and rippled, and jumped, as if a thousand sprites were holding unholy revel in the midnight hours; how it fascinated, charmed, enthralled, and carried the listeners out of themselves away from the concert room into the wild Hungarian hills into the very haunts of the pixies themselves. Then there came a hush in the music, a strange and solemn hush, out of which arose the luring voice of a single violin called forth by some master hand to utter its song of melody and love. Like the notes of a bird in the early morning, when awaking to life and sunshine, it pours forth a hymn of welcome, so the glad music of the violin danced and rippled over the stillness, until with one long drawn-out note of exquisite beauty it paused and all was stillness again. In the midst of the burst of applause which followed, Connisterre left his seat and went out to watch the play. The rooms, of course, were crowded. Not a vacant chair at any of the tables, while rows of people two or three deep screened the players from view. No sound save the whirling of the roulette ball and the hoarse voices of the croupiers——

'Le jeu est fait, messieurs,' or the rake, rake of the gold upon the cloth as fortunes were made or lost, and men and women, steeped to the lips in vice, leaned with hungry, covetous eyes over the tables, lost to everything save the sickening suspense of the moment and the adverse fate which whirled away their gains. Connisterre moved about from place to place as an aimless fancy dictated to him, occasionally staking some small amount, and winning or losing with equal indifference. The play had small fascination for him, although years ago it had fixed its talon-clutches upon his life for a season, but he could pity the helpless creatures who found themselves enchained like another Andromeda to the rock of play. It was during one of these temporary pauses to watch the result of a small stake of his own, that Connisterre found himself standing behind the chair of a young man who was losing heavily. Accustomed as any frequenter of Monte Carlo must be to see large sums lost with impassive indifference, the extreme agitation manifested by this player attracted Geoffrey's attention. The chair upon which he sat vibrated visibly, while his boyish face paled or reddened according as the fluctuations of the game were in his favour or the reverse.

For a time it seemed as if the luck had turned and was with him, then suddenly Dame

Caprice turned her back and he lost again
—lost all which he had won. Nothing remained now to the unfortunate player but one
solitary *louis*. This, after a momentary hesitation, he changed into two smaller coins,
staking one with trembling fingers. The
ball spun merrily round. Again he lost.
There was but one coin with which to retrieve his fallen fortunes.

He staked once more, this time deserting
the colour to which he had clung with such
odd persistence. Fate was still against him,
and he lost. With an imprecation upon lips
which had lost every vestige of colour, the
unfortunate man jumped up and left the table.
Immediately another took his place, eager to
run a tilt with fortune. Connisterre's eyes
followed the tall young figure with some compassion until it was lost among the crowd of
loiterers. A sickening disgust for the whole
scene had taken possession of him; the
heated rooms and scented air seemed over-
powering. Five minutes later he was out in

the Casino garden inhaling the pure night breeze with a sense of relief and refreshment. For some time he paced up and down the dusky paths, pursuing a train of reflection which, as was natural, had his unfortunate little protégée for its subject. He had by no means yet arrived at any solution of the problem as to what must eventually become of the girl if her husband could not be found. It was while he was strolling about between the myrtle hedges, which exhaled an almost sickly fragrance, that the sound of a long-drawn sigh startled Geoffrey from his reverie. He turned his head, making out in the dim light the outline of a man's form crouched upon a bench a couple of yards away, his head buried upon his folded arms, abject misery and despair depicted in every line of the stooping figure. Intuition, rather than knowledge, told Connisterre that he saw before him the man of whose losses he had been a witness half an hour before. Acting upon an impulse which the memory of his own

fatal experiences years before in this very
place aroused, he turned aside from the
path, and, sitting down upon the bench,
laid a kindly hand on the young man's
arm.

'Look here,' he said rather bluntly, 'I
think you had a facer just now in that cursed
hole.   Can I help you?'

Startled by Connisterre's voice the boy—
he was little more—turned round and faced
him.

'I beg your pardon,' he said in a thick,
dull voice.   'You spoke to me?'

'I asked if I could be of any service.   I
was—excuse me—an observer of your losses
at the table.'

'Loss,' echoed the boy bitterly.   'Ruin
would be a better word;' and then he turned
away again, shielding his face from Geoffrey's
scrutiny.

'Come, my lad,' said the other kindly.
'You are very young, too young for the
tables, I should have thought; but what is

done cannot be undone. Let us face the matter. What did you lose?'

'£250.'

A low whistle from Connisterre.

'Lost it all to-night?'

'Every cent.'

'Was the money yours?'

'What the devil does it signify to you whose it was?' exclaimed the young man, jumping to his feet as if the chance shot had gone home. 'I suppose it was not yours anyway? Kindly select one path and I will take another. I want neither your company nor your advice.'

The angry blood mounted to Connisterre's brow. Few men could submit tamely to such an insult.

'As you please, of course,' he said haughtily, and picking up the stick which had fallen from his hand, he strode away. But he had not gone many steps before conscience began to argue with him. At first he put the whisper aside. It was no concern of his if the young puppy chose to go to ruin. He had offered assistance which had been insolently refused. There was no further call upon him.

'I am not my brother's keeper,' he said, standing still and striking his stick rather savagely on the well-kept path. 'Probably the fool has only received what he well merited. It is not my business, so why should I lay myself open to any further impertinence.'

A pause. The night breeze came to him laden with the fragrance of roses and myrtle. Above him, glittering with light, the Casino looked down on the silent garden. Up there —vice, infamy, ruin, and shame. Down here in the lonely solitude its awful results. Connisterre looked back the way he had come. The impulse to return was almost irresistible. He remembered so vividly his own extremity in these very gardens; could he now cast it aside and leave a fellow-creature to ruin, when perhaps a timely word of counsel, some material help which he had it in his power to offer would avert it? The battle between pride and conscience was sharp, but it ended as all such battles must end with a man of Connisterre's sensitive calibre. The emotional side of his nature came uppermost, and, acting under its influence, he went back to his late companion, who had resumed his former position.

'Now,' said Geoffrey frankly, 'I have not the faintest shadow of right to interfere in your affairs, and if I were not actuated by a friendly interest my doing so would be an impertinence. I know what it is to lose money in that hole. I lost heavily myself once some years ago. Come, let me help you.'

'I don't see how you can,' said the other sullenly, but there was a wavering in voice and manner which Geoffrey's keen eye detected.

'Will you let me try?' he said, sitting down beside him. 'You have lost, you say, £250. Well, it is a large sum to fool away on nothing, but not too large to replace. Is that all?'

'All? Yes, and quite enough too considering it was not mine.' The truth was out now, blurted out involuntarily under stress of shame and excitement.

'You are staying here, I suppose?'

'I arrived this afternoon.'

'From where?'

'England.'

His confession did not take long. The facts, as stated by Quentin Lee—this was the name which the unfortunate young man gave to Connisterre—appeared to be simply these. He had, it seemed, been sent out by a London firm of stockbrokers to pay to a lady resident in Turin the sum of £250, a half-yearly instalment of an annuity due to her. This old lady, full of crotchets and peculiarities, strongly objected to receive her money in any other form than English notes and gold. It was a curious fad, but the firm, to a member of whom she was related, were willing to humour her. Accordingly every half-year the money was sent out to Turin by the hands of a confidential clerk. During the absence through illness of the responsible person usually entrusted with the conveyance of Miss Blumenthal's annuity, Quentin Lee had been sent off on this mission. Now, why Mr. Lee had chosen to come round by Monte Carlo instead of proceeding direct to Turin was best known to himself; but Connisterre saw no reason to disbelieve the young man's statement that he had gone there simply to try his luck with a little money of his own, and it was not until in a moment of madness he had staked away that furnished him by the firm for his travelling and hotel expenses, that the horrible temptation to try and retrieve his fortunes by the fraudulent use of Miss Blumenthal's money assailed him. What followed Connisterre already knew. It was useless to blame or make any words about the matter now. Men have yielded to sin before, they will do so again, and in Lee's present state of mind lay retribution fierce and strong.

'Have you any parents, Mr. Lee,' asked Connisterre, after he had listened in silence to the details of this shameful story.

'No.'

'Nor brother nor sister?'

'No.'

'Where do you live?'

'In rooms. How is a man to keep straight when nobody in the world cares a hang for him,' said Lee recklessly. 'Of acquaintances I have shoals; but you know, if you know anything of London life, what that means sometimes and to what it leads.'

'Yes, I know something of it. My name is Connisterre, Geoffrey Connisterre.'

'Not the artist, surely?' exclaimed the other, turning round upon him.

'Yes.'

'Then I owe you an apology for my bearishness,' said Lee. I had no idea to whom I was speaking. Thank you for all your kindness, Mr. Connisterre, but I am beyond any help now.'

As matters then stood he spoke truly. In the Casino bank lay Miss Blumenthal's £250, and before Quentin Lee the grim shadow of social ruin and a felony prosecution.

'Not quite so bad as that.'

'It could not well be worse. Look here, Mr. Connisterre, I give you my word, I never intended to touch the money.'

The honest, boyish tone carried conviction with it. Connisterre believed him.

'I daresay not. How did it begin?'

'By staking a five franc piece for luck,' he groaned. 'And I won, and won again. Then—I lost.'

'The old story! Well, it is a pity you hadn't the common sense to stop when you had lost only your own money.'

'And how was I to get to Turin?' retorted Lee fiercely. 'I had staked the money given me for travelling expenses.'

'You should have had sufficient moral courage to write to your employers and abide by the results. Serious they might have been, but not so serious as this.'

'But I expected to win.'

'Ah yes; we all do that,' said Connisterre drily. 'Most people fancy that fortunes are easily gained at Monte Carlo. However, it is no use saying any more. "Might have beens" won't help us. You have had a lesson which should be severe enough to teach you something. The question is now—Are you willing to give up the very doubtful pleasures of gaming for the future?'

'I shall be obliged. They don't give one *roulette* and *rouge et noir* at Dartmoor,' said Lee with a hard laugh.

'It need not be Dartmoor.'

'It must if I return to England.'

'I will save you from it, but on this one condition only. Give up gambling, and I lend you money to replace what you have lost.'

'*You will lend me the money?*' Then the pent-up emotion had its way. The revulsion of feeling to intense relief from an agony of despair was too much for Quentin Lee. Putting his head upon his arms, he broke down and cried like a child.

Connisterre looked round apprehensively, afraid they might be observed.

'Come, come,' he said, laying his hand gently as a brother might have done upon the heaving shoulder. 'Pull yourself together, Mr. Lee. I want you to fully understand the conditions upon which I lend you this money. I say *lend*, because I cannot afford to give it you.'

'You may trust me, it shall be paid back,' returned Lee in a voice choked with emotion. 'Only lend it to me, and I swear to pay you every farthing in time—but perhaps you cannot wait.'

'It is not a question of time; that to a certain extent I must leave in your hands. I have only the one condition to make. You give up play.'

'You need not urge that upon me. I will leave Monte Carlo to-morrow.'

'But leaving Monte Carlo is not every-thing, I say,' and Connisterre's voice grew very stern. 'I say, *give up play of every kind ;* that is, playing for gain. You are not firm enough yet to dabble with temptation, neither are you rich enough to waste your money if you must pay me back what I am lending you. Besides, remember this'—tightening his grip on Lee's arm—'you will never go nearer ruin than you have to-night. Let it be a warning to you, and if some time you are tempted to stake even so much as a six-pence upon the throw of a dice, just pause and think for a moment what your future would have been but for my being here to-night. I don't want any thanks. I would rather not have them. Give me your promise.'

'My word of honour is not worth much

now, but I promise all the same,' said Quentin Lee shamefacedly.   Then he struck his hand into Connisterre's, gripping it with almost painful force.

'As there is a God in heaven,' he went on in a low voice, 'I am yours, body and soul, from this moment. If the day ever comes when I can be of help, you will find that Quentin Lee's friendship is not to be despised.'

He meant it, meant every word of that hot, impetuous avowal, but how little either of them dreamed of the short time which would elapse before Quentin would be called upon to fulfil his vow, or the awful circumstances which would call it forth.

CHAPTER IX

INTO THE NEW WORLD

And God be with you whither you walk or ride ;
I must go on whither I have to go.—CHAUCER.

THE last services had been rendered to the
dead. The old life was over, a new one
must begin, and Léonie Connisterre, standing by that new-made grave in the pretty
Mentone cemetery, realised with a sudden
sickening sense of despair that what had
seemed but a hideous nightmare of the last
few days was a stern reality now. Alone,
friendless, dependent for charity upon a man
of whose existence she had been twenty-four
hours ago totally ignorant, fearful of every
future step, not daring to remain, yet dread-
ing to go forward, no wonder that the girlish
face, sharpened by anxiety, bore such a look

of dread, such a look indeed, that all the manly, chivalrous pity in Connisterre's nature warmed into sudden life.

'My poor child,' he exclaimed impetuously as they stood side by side looking down upon the flower-laden coffin at their feet. 'I wish I could say something to comfort you, something to convince you that under my care you are as safe as if you were with your brother. By the memory of the dead lying here—and surely a man can take no more solemn oath than this—I swear no harm shall come to you that I can avert while you are under my protection. Cannot you trust me?'

'I must trust you,' she said drearily; 'only I am afraid of the future—I don't know what to do. I am so lonely, and if Gerard does not come back there is nobody to give me a home.'

Tears were brimming over in the big dark eyes, but she forced them back with a resolute effort, and turning away from her companion, knelt down by the grave, pressing her lips passionately to a rose, which had fallen from one of the wreaths, and lay upon the freshly turned mould.

'Good-bye, good-bye, dear!' she murmured in a whisper. 'I must leave you now, but I shall never forget you. Do you know how very lonely I am here?'

Connisterre waited a moment, then touched her shoulder gently.

'Don't think me a brute,' he said, 'but you—must come now, my poor child.'

Léonie got up obediently.

'Yes, I am quite ready,' she said with a little sob, and then they went away together. Later on that same day, when Connisterre and the girl who had been thrown so curiously on his protection had left Monte Carlo, a fiacre drove up to the front of the Hotel de la Torre. Of the two men it contained, one was much younger than the other, a medium height, fair-haired, Saxon type of man, with an average share of good looks, somewhat marred by a sullen expression which pervaded

the whole face, and lay like a shadow in the
blue gray eyes. The other, older and lighter,
was essentially Russian in type of counten-
ance, but from dress, speech, and manner,
might pass anywhere for an Englishman.
Only the eyes betrayed something of the
undercurrents of passion beneath that calm
exterior. Keen, watchful, always on the
alert, they seemed to scintillate like diamonds
under the level brows.

'I suppose if they have left you will go back
to Venice,' he was saying to his companion, as
the fiacre stopped and two waiters came out.

'Back to Venice and on to Alexandria, I
think,' was the surly response.

'Come to St. Petersburg with me.'

'You and St. Petersburg and the whole
realm of the Czar be hanged,' returned the
fair man explosively, and he jumped out of
the carriage. 'Garçon, is M. Deane still
here? Tell him that M. Connisterre has
come, and has only half an hour to spare.
Look sharp now, and don't stand gaping

there at me like a Chinese idol. Are you
coming in, Neudroschky, or going to the
Casino,' he added, turning to his companion.

'Coming in, I think — if I do not em-
barrass you by making a third at this pleasant
little interview.'

By this time Monsieur Delaney, summoned
to the spot by one of the waiters who, perhaps, preferred to shift the onus of the explanation on the shoulders of his superior, had
made his appearance. Then arose confusion,
bewildered questions, strong language from
the fair man, and satirical laughter from his
companion.

'If you mean this for a joke,' began
Gerard Connisterre fiercely; but Monsieur Delaney repeated his statement with
unruffled politeness.

M. Deane was dead, had been buried that
morning at Mentone. Madame, his daughter,
left immediately afterwards with a gentleman,
presumably her husband, who had arrived
the previous day, and gave his name as M.

Connisterre. Also he had paid certain expenses connected with the funeral arrangements, and taken charge of all madame's
affairs. Pressed to describe the stranger,
Monsieur Delaney hesitated.

'Monsieur, he was not unlike you. A little
taller perhaps, but the same eyes, hair, and
complexion, possibly a shade darker, but
otherwise he would pass for your brother
easily.'

'But the girl is *my* wife,' exclaimed the
new comer, banging his hand with some
violence upon the table.

Monsieur Delaney shrugged his shoulders.
Possibly he thought madame was to be
congratulated upon her escape from such a
very hot-tempered master.

'That is as it may be,' he returned with a
little bow. 'The other, he also gave me to
understand that he had a legal claim, and I
saw no reason to doubt him. Madame is
fortunate in that she has so many cavaliers.
It is not every——'

'Curse your insolence,' exclaimed Gerard Connisterre fiercely.

'*Mon ami*, there is nothing gained by such violence,' said the Russian, laying his hand upon the other's arm. 'This marriage it has been hateful to you—free yourself now if you will, only remember,' he dropped his voice to a whisper, and spoke in Russian, 'there is the publicity to fear. Follow the love birds if it so pleases you — but I would suggest——'

'Save yourself the trouble of suggesting anything,' returned Gerard sullenly. 'I shall not move one single step after her. She may go to the devil if she likes, and he with her. Damn them both.'

The young man turned away and went out into the sunshine again. Neudroschky followed him, rolling a cigarette between his fingers. The fiacre was still waiting for them.

'I am at your service, *mon ami*,' said the Russian imperturbably. 'Shall we go back to Venice?'

'Go where you like.' Connisterre jumped in and jammed his hat lower over his brows. Neudroschky got in after him.

'It is well,' he said, leaning back. 'You are saved the pain of an interview, and I the boredom of being present at it. Adieu, Monte Carlo!'

CHAPTER X

GOOD-BYE

Thus may she perish who once wore that ring !
Thus do I spurn her from me ; do thus trample
Her memory in the dust !

The Spanish Student.

ROME, the Eternal City, enthroned upon her
seven hills ; Rome, hot, sunshiny, full of
noise and glare, bustle, confusion, fiacre
drivers, and pretty flower-girls. The foun-
tains were splashing merrily away in the
piazzas, cooling the air with huge jets of
water which spouted from the mouths of re-
cumbent lions, and fell with a rhythmical
splash and gurgle over the backs of baby
Tritons, gambolling in the massive stone
basins below. All afternoon the sun had
been streaming down on the steps of the

Piazza di Spagna, and over the picturesque beggars in their dirt and rags, lying sleeping there in lazy content, oblivious either of the intense heat, or the foot passengers climbing painfully up step by step towards the little church of Trinità dei Monti at the summit. The sky, blue as only an Italian sky can be, was almost wearying in its monotony; not a cloud, not even a fleck of white to break the azure as it lay like a canopy miles above the sunlit city. Crowds of people, taking advantage of a slight breeze which had sprung up as the afternoon drew to a close, were streaming towards the Pincian hill, in the wake of royalty. Dark-eyed Italian officers, tourist Englishmen, pretty women in carriages, all the wealth and beauty and life of Rome mingling together in that fashionable promenade, where the strains of the band floated out into the perfumed air, and all was mirth and gaiety.

Just far enough away from the Pincian hill to be out of earshot of its music, but not

of the roar and rattle of the carriages wending
their way towards it, two people, a man and
a woman, were standing in a private sitting-
room of a large hotel.   The windows were
thrown wide open, and from here one could
gaze down into the animated scene below.
Little cared either of those two actors in
the drama for anything outside.   The sun
streamed gaily in over the pretty furniture,
the flowers and fruit decorating the table,
over Geoffrey Connisterre's hot, indignant
face, and the graceful figure of the woman
opposite to him.   She was standing by the
table, one hand resting upon its polished
surface, the other holding a bunch of roses
to the breast of her pretty summer dress,
which was so white and delicate that it had
almost a bridal effect in its simplicity.   A
lovely woman some might say, an unapproach-
able one would most, but even Claudia Desborough's slow pulses had been stirred, and
her face, usually so passionless, was pale now
with outraged pride and dignity.

'You *cannot* deny it!' she said in a quick, excited voice, retreating a step as he came nearer to her. 'You dare not deny it! and yet you have the audacity to come here and plead as your excuse that — but I will not repeat it—I will not listen to another———'

'You shall!' thundered Geoffrey, his face crimson with anger. 'You shall hear my explanation, and tell me also who has brought this slanderous tale to your ears! In justice to yourself—to me, Claudia, tell me who it is?' There was a pleading note in the deep voice, but Claudia flung up her head haughtily.

'I decline to answer. Were you or were you not at Monte Carlo the day upon which you had told me I was to expect you here?'

'I was unexpectedly summoned there!'

She made a little disdainful movement, letting the bunch of roses fall unheeded to the floor.

'You were there under circumstances not fit to be mentioned between us.'

'I wonder—did you ever care for me,

Claudia ?' Connisterre asked, leaning heavily against the table. 'If you did, surely the love is not worth much which fails to stand the test of a false story—a hateful slander, and refuses me even a patient hearing or the benefit of a doubt——'

'And what explanation could you offer which would not lower my self-respect to hear,' she broke in, a quick flash of resentment in her blue eyes.

'You will not allow me to speak,' he said quietly.

'I have heard enough. Here is your ring, Mr. Connisterre, I have done with it—and you.' She removed the little diamond circlet from her finger and laid it between them on the table.

'Day after day, when surely courtesy alone might have brought you here, you lingered on in Venice, leaving me to endure the wonderment and sarcasm of my friends that you could delay your arrival so long without any adequate reason. And now you would have me believe that this impromptu journey to Monte Carlo was the outcome of a strange coincidence of names, that you went there under a misapprehension, and were by force of circumstances obliged to assume the responsibilities of another man. I am to credit that she is a stranger, this girl with whom you were masquerading at Monte Carlo. It is monstrous, shameful. How dare you expect me to discuss such matters with you?'

'I don't!' exclaimed Geoffrey, the veins on his forehead standing out like whipcord; and he dashed his hand with such a fury of passion upon the table that Claudia started nervously back, while the ring, displaced by his anger, rolled away and fell upon the carpet at their feet. 'I don't expect you after this revelation of a want of faith to believe a single word I say. The loss of such a love as yours is nothing since you will take before *my* word, that of some wretched scandalmonger whose only wish is to sow dissension between you and me. Had

you asked that I should have faith in *your*
truth, and honour, and purity, even if
circumstances were against you and it was
out of your power to explain, should I ever
have doubted *you*? And yet although I
come now, with a full and frank explanation
upon my lips, anxious to clear away and set
right this damning story, you will not listen,
you affect to disbelieve me, you return scorn
for candour. You are pitiless as a stone.'

For an instant the girl's dark blue eyes
wavered, the hard lines about her mouth
softened. Surely so, or else it was fancy
upon Geoffrey's part. He went a little
nearer to her, and his voice dropped to a
supplicating whisper.

'Claudia, you *do* believe me?'

A moment's pause.

'No,' she said at last, and she moved away
from him. 'I do *not*.'

The hot blood swept in scorching tide
into Connisterre's face. Outraged pride
crushed down with an iron hand what a

moment before had been a whole wealth of love and tender entreaty, his lips tightened into a straight line beneath his fair moustache. ' Very well,' he said, drawing a long breath ; 'that is your last word ; now listen to mine.' With an angry gesture he stamped his foot upon the ring at his feet—

' As there is a heaven above I will never sue to you for love or favour again. From this day let us be strangers to one another. I at least shall not try to overstep the boundary.'

Without waiting for another word, without even a backward glance at the face of the woman who, for a time at all events, had made the brightness of his life, coloured all his future, and gilded the dream of his artistic ambitions, Connisterre left the hotel, hardly conscious what he did or where he went, his heart ablaze with a concentrated passion which, after the first few minutes, startled him by the power it had assumed. Every nerve was quivering, strung up to its highest tension

from the excitement of the late interview and
Claudia's unmerited scorn.   Never through-
out the whole of his life had Connisterre's
hot temper so thoroughly mastered him, and
if at this moment the man who had been the
cause of this unhappy rupture had come in
his path, who can say what the result of that
meeting might have been.   Walking quickly
on, looking neither to the right nor left,
Geoffrey found himself at length in the
grateful solitude of the grounds of the Villa
Borghesi.   A few people were strolling
about, but so spacious is the park that
any one wishful to escape from his fellow-
creatures and seek retirement may easily
find the opportunity.   Here, stretched full
length upon the short velvety turf, gazing
blankly at the dancing, quivering leaves above
his head, and the eternal blue sky peeping
down between the interlaced branches of the
trees, Connisterre fell into a moody reverie.
The first violence of his passion had subsided,
lulled insensibly by the soothing voice of

nature speaking to him out of the exquisite tender beauty of the afternoon, and little by little he began to realise what all this meant to him. Life was not by any means over because one woman had played him false, not over, oh no ; but for a time at least it was very dark and gloomy. He had to realise that the chief interest in his life was removed, that his ambitious hopes, which hitherto had centred round Claudia Desborough, must for the future feed upon themselves. That she had—well there was nothing gained by disguising the truth to himself—*deliberately thrown him over.* A nine days' wonder, that was all. Lying there in his solitude, Connisterre fancied he could hear the remarks of his own particular artistic set when this piece of news was wafted to them, and he ground his teeth as he listened to the fragments of mental conversation carried on within his brain.

'It is all off between Connisterre and Miss Desborough?'

'So I suppose. Any one know why?'

'Oh, the old story! He hadn't enough money.'

' Not a bit of it. Another woman; and the fair Claudia does not like divided honours.'

' Early days to try that on. Should have waited until the knot was tied——' and so on —so on.

Connisterre leaned his head upon his hand and reviewed the details of this brief engagement of his. He remembered Claudia as he had seen her first the previous May, at one of the gayest of gay London balls; remembered how his artistic senses had been charmed, and his eyes fascinated by the girl's exquisite face and figure, her almost regal gait, the flowing yellow draperies suiting so well that coronet of curling hair which seemed as if it had been dusted over with bronze, the proud self-controlled lips, the faultless curve of neck and shoulders.

' She is like a goddess,' he had said to his friend Austin Kavanagh, as they stood beside an open door, looking towards Claudia

Desborough with her little court of wor-
shippers, and Austin had laughed.

'True, oh king! Fair as a goddess and
heartless as the marble out of which she is
sculptured. Too much of the deity, too
little of the woman for love.'

Had Austin been right? Connisterre
plucked restlessly at the velvety turf. No,
he was not prepared to admit that, even if his
ardent affection had been powerless to move
Claudia to a corresponding warmth. Such
love as lay in her nature he believed had
been given to him, asking not in return that
he should lavish upon her the devotion which
it was beyond his power to control. He had
loved her, poor fool, from that first moment of
introduction, down through the days of their
brief engagement to the present, when, for a
momentary disbelief which cut at the root of
all his honour, and shamed them both, she
had flung him back upon himself. But pride
counted for an important factor in Connisterre's
nature. There would be no wearing of the

willow on his part, no effort for reconciliation, no look, nor word, nor sigh to recall the past. He had done with Claudia for ever; but as he sat there in the glad sunshine, heedless of the carolling birds and the beauty which surrounded him, something undoubtedly died in the man's hitherto generous and affectionate nature—a little of his better self, a fragment of the love and faith and charity which had formed so large an element in his disposition. He was the same and yet not quite the same, for sometimes the breaking up of our cherished idols is apt to leave a stamp of the devil upon us.

CHAPTER XI

LÉONIE

Alas ! what wonder is it that she wept,
Sent to a strange land and a cloudy fate.
                                            Canterbury Tales.

'La pauvre petite? No, Monsieur Connisterre. It is that she has gone to the Campo Santo for a little promenade—a little change. Ah, she is so *triste*, the child; my heart it aches for her.'

Such was the response given to Connisterre two days later, when upon arriving in Genoa he made his way to the little old-fashioned house where he had left Léonie some days previously, and inquired for her.

'Then I must try to find her there,' he said, hesitating at the open door.

'But not just now—this very moment,'

urged Madame Réclamier. 'You will take one little cup of coffee with me, monsieur, n'est-ce pas?'

Connisterre looked at his watch.

'Thank you, yes,' he said, yielding to her solicitations. He knew that it would give the sisters a real pleasure for him to accept their hospitality, to admire their flowers, and their cats, and the queer ill-shapen little house which had been their home for so many years. So he went in and drank the excellent coffee prepared by Madame Réclamier's wrinkled hands, and enjoyed the rest after his dusty journey. He had a great regard for these two old sisters, who were living out what remained of their sinless lives in that once powerful city of Genoa, and practising such charities as their limited resources permitted amongst the poor and fallen in her streets.

Nobody knew better than Connisterre the kindliness and generosity which Madame Réclamier and her sister were willing to offer when any poor creature came to them in distress, and he had felt perfectly contented to leave Léonie in their charge.

'The poor child has not heard from her husband, then?' he said, stirring his coffee as he sat in the low window which commanded a view of a busy street leading down to the quay.

'No; not even one little note,' returned the vivacious Frenchwoman, shrugging her shoulders. She say to me, 'Mademoiselle Thérèse, what is it that I must do? I have no money, no home, no friend. I would work, but I can find no work.'

'There is no hurry for it,' interrupted Connisterre. 'I will do what I can for her if that scoundrel does not turn up.'

'So I tell her. I beseech that she will be at rest. I say, "Ma petite, Monsieur Connisterre, he has the good heart of an angel. He will help you. He will be decide."'

'And yet it is very difficult for a man in my position to do so. If I take charge of her future I must be prepared to risk the strictures of a gossiping world,' said Connisterre gloomily. 'Mrs. Grundy, as we in England term her, has a tongue like a two-edged sword, madame.'

'You are right, you are right, monsieur ; it is indeed a sorrowful world. There is but little shelter for the innocent when once the dark bird of scandal drops his feathers over them. May the blessed saints have her under their protection. You do not know where he is, monsieur le mari ?'

'I wish I did,' said Connisterre, with an ugly look. Then he rose and put down his cup.

'I will take a stroll round the city until this little wanderer returns, or perhaps I might get so far as the Campo Santo ; I don't know,' he said.

Outside in the sunlit street, however, Geoffrey turned at once in the direction of the Campo Santo. He knew every foot of Genoa, its ghostly palaces and gilded

churches; he was familiar with its crooked
street and bye-ways, and every inch of the
huge harbour, for he had spent in his boyish
days hour after hour watching the mighty
ships as they steamed in and out. There
was no tourist-like curiosity now to draw
him on the road of sightseers. Perhaps
the best way of spending the afternoon
would be to do as he had first proposed
and follow Léonie. There was just a chance
that he might come across her there, and if
so, time and place would be eminently suited
for the interview which was to decide so much.
He had a great deal to say to her, something
also to suggest. Even in the midst of his
anxieties of the last few days he had found
time to think of Léonie and her position, and
had gone even so far as to inquire about a
suitable home for her in England should
Gerard Connisterre not be forthcoming.

Advertisements in guarded terms had been
inserted in all the leading papers with a view
to bringing the wanderer back, but so far no

success followed their appearance.　Geoffrey shrewdly suspected the man was keeping dark, wishful to avoid the responsibilities which Mr. Deane's death had brought upon him, and he admitted a little ruefully that the part of knight-errant under these circumstances was an embarrassing one to play.　There was, however, some compensation for all his trouble in Léonie's unfeigned delight when they met in one of the corridors of the Campo Santo. He came up to her unobserved, for the girl, absorbed in contemplation of the exquisitely sculptured figure of a woman lying asleep at the foot of a cross, a bunch of poppy heads in her hand, did not hear his footsteps echoing along the marble pavement.

'C'est vous, c'est vous, monsieur,' she exclaimed ecstatically, seizing both his hands, her queer little face radiant with smiles, 'voulez-vous donnez moi——'

'Will *you* speak English,' he said laughing.　'You must learn to be as fluent in your native tongue as you are in your adopted one, mademoiselle — madame, I mean.'

She made a little grimace, but obeyed, rattling on excitedly about Genoa, and the maiden sisters, and her delight at seeing him, while Connisterre stood patiently listening, half-touched, half-amused. Léonie spoke English fairly well, now and then coming to a full stop for want of the requisite word, or turning a sentence in some odd fashion which, however, literally interpreted her meaning. It was a barbarous tongue, a very barbarous tongue, she averred.

'I have been trying to make one plan, one little plan,' she said looking up at him rather wistfully. 'You know my husband—he is not returned——'

'I also have a plan,' Connisterre interrupted; 'but before we discuss either yours or mine, I think you must treat me quite as a friend. My dear little girl I do not wish to force your confidence—far from that. What you desire to keep secret I will never try to learn ; but you see at present I am working in the dark. If I am to advise or help, you on your part must make the way easier.'

' You mean——'

' That if you feel at liberty to tell me any-thing respecting the past, your husband, and his reason for deserting you, it will be a great assistance to me in determining what is best to be done,' Geoffrey said steadily.

Léonie looked away from him down the lonely corridor. A streak of sunlight had flickered in from the further end and was dancing incongruously over the monuments of death. He watched the proud, sensitive face in silence, and found himself wondering if the girl had any pretensions to beauty. Yes, he decided she had, but where did they lie ? Was it in the bright chestnut hair which she wore in a loose knot at the back of her small head, the dark eyes under their faintly pencilled brows, the small *retroussé* nose, the mouth with its white irregular teeth, the firm, not to say, obstinate little chin, slightly pointing upwards? No, taking them feature by feature not in any of these, for each more or less defied the laws of feminine beauty, but rather in a sort of gipsyish wilfulness of expression which pervaded all, and would probably become more apparent when grief for the loss of her father had grown less poignant, and permitted her natural disposition to assert itself. She was not an easy girl to manage, Connisterre felt sure of that, not a gentle, clinging, dependent little creature who would be content to take the decision of others as final. There was a very volcano of passion in those big dark eyes and mutinous lips, nervous excitement and demonstrativeness in the small slender hands. She turned her face towards him at last, a satirical smile just curving her lips.

'Oh, you are right. But what am I to tell? Can you not help me without?'

'I can,' he said slowly.

'But you do not wish?'

'I would rather not work so much in

the dark.   Come, Léonie—I may call you Léonie, you are but a child.   Don't you think I have earned a partial right to your confidence?   I have shown that I am to be trusted.'

'You are all that is kind and generous,' she said, with a sudden burst of feeling.   'It is I who am wrong and ungrateful.   Oh, I wish I could help myself.'

'Have you always lived abroad?' asked Connisterre, thinking he might possibly gain his end better by dint of skilful questioning.

'Always!'

'But your father?   He was an Englishman?'

'And my mother an Italian.   Yes.   We were Bohemians, gipsies, what you will, but do not blame my father.   It is always that he did what was kind for me, and if sometimes we were rich, and sometimes we were poor, it only hurt ourselves.'

Connisterre began to suspect that the late Mr. Deane had been one of those gambling

spendthrifts who infest most Continental
cities, and eke out a precarious living by
more or less dishonourable means. If so,
had he used his young daughter as a decoy
duck? The idea was distinctly unpleasing.
He held his peace, and waited for more.

'My mother died when I was quite a
little one,' the girl went on, with suddenly
softening eyes.   'Ah, la povera madre!'

'And has she no relations who would give
you shelter?'

'I do not know. I do not care.'

'And your father?'

'He said that he did quarrel with them,'
Léonie returned, in a low, rather ashamed
tone.

'Which stops the way there then. And
now about this other man, your husband.
What of him; he is an Englishman?'

'English, yes; and a little, just a little,
like you. 'Can it be,' this very hopefully,
'that he may be your brother, monsieur?'

'I have no brother, and I am sure he

is not a cousin. I do not believe that
my father had any married brother. The
similarity of names is just a coincidence,
probably. Had you known your husband
some time before you married him, Léonie?'

'One month and a half.'

'One month and—six weeks you mean.
Great Heaven! what was your father thinking about to let you marry a man of whom
you knew so little?'

'But we saw him at often times,' she
protested with a pout. 'He did come to
our rooms in Homburg to play cards, and I
liked him then. He was kind and *intéressant, très intéressant.*'

'Yes.' Connisterre's suspicions gathered
force.

'Then one day he did say, would I marry
him?'

'And you cared enough for him to say
yes?'

Léonie nodded her head.

'Daddie wished it; he asked that I would

marry Monsieur Connisterre, so I did not see
why I must say no. We were married do
you say? at Homburg.'

'But surely you knew something about
him—his family or his life?'

'I did know *nothing*,' she said, brushing
her hair back with a tired gesture. 'He
said one day that he was quite alone in the
world, for his father many many years ago
had quarrelled with his family.'

'And so you just lived on in Homburg for
how long after you were married?'

'Three months.'

'And then?'

'Then he left me.'

'Left you. Why?'

A slow fire of anger was gathering in
Léonie's expressive eyes.

'You ask too many questions,' she said,
flashing back a glance at him.

'You must not think it is impertinent
curiosity,' Connisterre returned very gently.
'I only wish to find out if there is a proba-

bility of his return before we decide anything definitely for the future.'

'Then I tell you this. He will *not* return. We quarrelled, or I mean that he did with my father, and I heard him say he would not come again. He said—but well, never mind what he did say,' she broke off, with a sudden glow of colour dyeing her cheeks. 'They were insulting words, they were a wicked slander.'

'And you overheard him?'

'Yes, I did; but he said to me, and oh! he was quite white with anger, that he had been deceived, and he would leave me. I said he might leave me if so he wished. I had my father, and I would be happy. But you see I did not think Gerard quite meant it all. I thought he was just angry because that he had lost money at the tables. He has never returned. I do not know where he is. That is a year ago.'

'And you have been living at Homburg all the time?'

'Not quite. We were often at Baden-
Baden, and sometimes Aix. It is six weeks
that we are at Monte Carlo when my father
was so ill. I could not think he must die,
but he said yes.'

Léonie brushed away her tears, speaking
with an evident effort to control the rising
emotion which threatened to overcome her.

'Yes,' said Geoffrey softly. 'And then
he wrote to your husband. Your father
must have known of his whereabouts.'

'Whereabouts?' she repeated inquiringly.

'His address. Where he was likely to be
found.'

'Yes I suppose so. One day, when I
was working a little beside him, he said that
now he was dying there would be no reason
why Gerard should not come back home.'

'What did he mean?'

'I do not know. He only said that he
would write—and you do know what it is
after. I mean what did come when you
found the letter.'

'And your father never told you what reason he had for believing your husband to be in Venice?'

' No.'

There was silence for some time. There is no doubt that to determine the multifarious motives which actuate weak human nature to a deed of evil one must possess the intuition of a God. Connisterre could only make a faint guess now at the circumstances of the case, but he had heard enough to feel assured that Léonie had been both wrongly and unfairly dealt with. Although he had no positive proof it was so, he felt convinced that Gerard Connisterre was keeping wilfully out of the way and persisting in the desertion of his wife. It was hardly probable that all the advertisements which Geoffrey had inserted in the papers could have failed to come under the other man's notice. That being so, the reason of the rupture must be only conjecture. Very possibly Gerard Connisterre had found his father-in-law out in some malpractices, or, to be quite plain, cardsharping, and had decided to cut himself free from this undesirable connection. Sooner than allow a discreditable story to come to the surface, Deane had consented to the separation. As to Léonie herself, Connisterre's nature revolted at the idea she could be in any way to blame. She was too young, too childish and unsophisticated, to have played the part of decoy duck to any great extent. He preferred to credit her with an innocent compliance rather than duplicity.

'Well, Léonie,' he said cheerfully, ' I will not ask you any more questions ; perhaps I have asked you too many already. It remains now to decide what is best to be done. We need not as yet give up the hope of hearing from your husband, but if in the course of a few days he does not write we must conclude that his return is improbable.'

' I do not think he will come back,' Léonie persisted, running her fingers over the marble hand of one of the statues.

'Very well. Let us suppose, then, that for a time you have to depend upon your own resources. Have you formed any plan for the future? What did your father advise?'

'He did not know,' said the girl mournfully. 'I think he hoped Gerard would come back. He just kept saying "Ma pauvre enfante, ma pauvre enfante," when he was conscious.'

'Is your husband in a position to provide for you? Has he money, I mean?'

'Money? Why yes some I think. But,' Léonie looked up with a flash of passionate anger in her eyes, 'I do not care how much money he has, or if he is as rich as a duke, I will never take one penny from him or eat his bread again. It would choke me. He may go his own way, and I will work that I may find money for myself.'

'And yet,' said Connisterre softly, mindful perhaps of his reception that embarrassing afternoon at Monaco, 'you would have been glad to see him a little while ago. Is it not so?'

'If he had come when I was lonely, just when my father died, yes. But now I am stronger I will learn to walk alone. Monsieur Connisterre, you are good; you will help me tó find some money.'

'Shall we go outside?' said Connisterre, touching her shoulder. 'You will be tired standing here so long. Also it is chilly, and I have a great deal to say to you.'

So they left the corridor with all its monuments to the sleeping dead, and went out into the sunshine, where, in default of a better resting-place, they sat down on one of the marble steps of the long flight which led up to the little circular chapel. Here, with the great God's acre stretching away before them, lonely and silent this summer day, Connisterre unfolded his plans.

'It is not easy for me to advise you,' he said, poking his stick into one of the crevices of the marble. 'You have never taken a dependent position, or worked for your living, and—candidly I do not think you will find it easy. Then another thing—I am ignorant of what qualifications you possess.'

'I can dance, and I can sing rather well,' said Léonie proudly.

'Yes?'

'And win a game of billiards against a good player. I don't play cards at all, father would not let me learn.'

Connisterre's heart gave a quick throb of relief.

'Then I can ride, too. Sometimes when we had more money we would hire horses and travel long rides in the morning. Ah!' clasping her hands ecstatically, 'it was beautiful. I think, perhaps, I might dance in the opera, monsieur? I do not know if there is any other way. What do English girls work when they have no money?'

'Upon my soul I don't know what English girls don't do except "'bus

conduct and collect taxes,"' said Connisterre rather savagely. 'They are ubiqui-
tous,—here, there, and everywhere. No profession, trade, nor amusement is safe from
their inroads. They teach and they preach,
they lecture and write, they study medicine
and science, they pull off university de-
grees over the heads of Oxford men ; in fact,
as I say, there is no limit to a woman's
ambition now. Perhaps it is a happier state
for them ; I don't know. The question remains—what are *you* to do ?'

'Indeed, I do not know,' said Léonie,
rather bewildered by Connisterre's rapid
English.

'Would you care for a berth as companion.
I know a lady with whom I think you could
be very happy.'

'Is she a friend of yours ?'

'Yes.'

'In London, where you live ?'

'No, a hundred miles away.'

'Then I think I would not love it,' returned this young Bohemian frankly. 'I like to be with you, and in that dirty, foggy England I am sure it will be very *triste* all alone. I will not be the very little piece of trouble to you, monsieur.'

'But, my dear child, I don't see that I can take charge of you,' said Connisterre, hardly knowing whether to be most amused or appalled by the extent of his responsibility. 'Of course, if you are not happy another post can be found for you, a companionship, or—or something of that kind. You will not be any worse off than hundreds of other girls who are obliged to face the world.'

'But will I know where you are?'

'You shall have my address.'

'Then I can run to you if I am not happy?'

'No certainly not.' The vision of Léonie arriving at some inconvenient moment in his old house on Campden Hill startled him. 'You must write. Sometimes I am not in London, and it would be risky to come looking for me. I told you I was an artist.'

'Yes. I wish I could see your pictures.'

'So you shall some day. Lady Paget, to whom I suggested you should go as companion, lives in Derbyshire. It is beautiful there, and they have a most picturesque old house.'

'And is it only Lady Paget?'

'No, she has a husband, and one daughter who takes a great interest in parish work.'

'What is parish work?'

'Oh, a sort of Lady Bountiful working amongst the poor. I daresay you would have to help her; at least Lady Paget gave me to understand this. Perhaps just at first you might not like either Miss Paget or Sir John, but we all have our little peculiarities, you know.'

Léonie made a wry face.

'I would like to travel with you,' she said calmly.

'But that is impossible. Lady Paget, who is at present in Rome will I know make you very happy. Her suggestion is that she should pick you up here on her way to England next week—that is, of course, if your husband does not come before then. She is willing to give you thirty pounds a year and pay all your travelling expenses. The salary does not seem much, but you are so inexperienced that you might have difficulty in obtaining a higher one.'

Connisterre did not say that it was only after a great deal of friendly entreaty that he had been able to persuade the baronet's wife into accepting Léonie in lieu of the very worthy and estimable young person with whom she was then in communication for the post. Lady Paget had in fact said very frankly, that she was by no means disposed to receive such a young Bohemian into her house, feeling pretty sure that matters would hardly run smoothly between Léonie and her daughter, who was the essence of decorum and propriety. But Connisterre had over-ruled all her objections, and pleaded so hard his protégée's friendless condition, that Lady

Paget, who, when left to herself, was very charitable, finally consented. Something of her acquiescence was no doubt owing to her wish to please Connisterre. Deep down in the old lady's innocently scheming brain, there lurked a hope that in time he and Monica might become more than the acquaintances they were at present; surely to refuse him a favour now was to throw an obstacle into her cherished plan.

'It is for you to decide,' said Connisterre at last, breaking in upon the reverie into which Léonie had fallen. 'Will you go?'

She turned a look upon him, such a look as one may see in the startled apprehensive eyes of a bird which beholds the open door of the cage into which it is to be forced. What matter that the bars are gilded and the groundsel fresh? It is a prison for all that, a dreary prison which knows not the name of freedom. Here was Léonie, a veritable wild bird of nature, asked of her own free will to assume the shackles of restraint, to accept a life of which she knew nothing, except that it meant the curtailment of her most precious heritage—liberty ; meant the dreary round of conventional decorum, the farewell to all that happy nomadic Bohemian life which, in spite of its poverty and anxieties, had been, oh, so happy!   Did Connisterre quite realise what he was asking her ?   The colour came and went like April sunshine in the vagabond little face, her eyes—but she had averted her eyes from his, and was gazing persistently at a tiny lizard darting about in the sunshine at their feet.

' I shall—I would have to be very respectable ? ' she queried at length, with a quiver of amusement in her voice, and a look of something not unlike *diablerie* in her face.

' Yes, I suppose you will,' he assented, rather lamely.

A long silence.   Only the carolling of a bird soaring higher and higher into the heavens, and the whisper of a summer breeze as it hurried by.   A butterfly fluttered upwards, pausing to rest a moment upon Léonie's sombre draperies, and make a vivid dab of colour there ; the lizard whisked back into his hole. Then came a faint clatter of feet on the marble steps behind. Somebody was coming out of the little chapel. Léonie gave a long, long sigh. Surely in it her heart went nigh to breaking, for even Connisterre could hardly guess what this decision meant to her.

'Yes, I will go to England,' she said, putting her slim hand in his. And then together they went back to the queer little house where Mademoiselle Thérèse was waiting for them.

CHAPTER XII

A HEEDLESS PAIR

Hang sorrow ! care will kill a cat,
And therefore let's be merry.

G. WITHER.

THE brilliancy of summer had faded somewhat, and already dame autumn's chilling
finger was laying a warning touch upon the
green and golden foliage of the dusky woods.
There was a grayness in the sky where it
touched the horizon and melted away indis-
tinctly into the meadow-land beyond, a whistle
in the voice of the wind as rising from its
hiding-place, it murmured a dreary song and
fled onwards through the forest, carrying
away in its grip a whole avalanche of fluttering bronze-tinted leaves which a touch of
frost had loosened from the parent stem.

The bracken, red and gold, was clothing the hill side like some gay tournament cloth spread abroad in gorgeous beauty, while a few late blackberries which had escaped the devastating hand of the pickers hung disconsolately on the hedge sides, or fell unnoticed into the deep dyke below. There was more than a whisper of death and decay in the chill air, more than a whisper of coming winter in the carpet of leaves lining the forest paths and giving back such a crisp rustle to the flying feet of the rabbits as they scuttered to and fro amongst the undergrowth. The sun, glowing like a round scarlet ball, hung low in the heavens, touching with ruddy beams the waving tree tops which raised their heads aloft, and the great purple hills outlined like a shadow against the sky behind them. Léonie Connisterre, nurtured under warm Italian skies, shivered a little as she raced on in the evening shadows, but there was a delicious freshness in the breeze, a keen, sharp sense of exhilaration which set all her blood tingling with a new enjoyment and sense of health. Quentin Lee, striding on beside her, his long steps hardly sufficing to keep pace with her flying feet, looked down at the flushed little face admiringly.

'You have a rattling good colour now,' he said, shifting the gun which he carried to his other arm, that he might help Léonie over a stile which barred their progress. 'A day like this, with just a touch of frost in the air, a sharp breeze sweeping over the downs, is better than any cosmetic in the world.'

'Except that it reddens one's nose,' said Léonie, rubbing the offending member with a vigour which intensified its already glowing colour. 'It is only in a novel that a girl's nose does not become red when the wind is in the east.'

'The wind is not east, it is north,' said Lee, argumentatively. 'I noticed the weather-vane on the church spire as we came past. If it were east you and I would not be enjoy-

ing the walk so much.   You know the old
couplet—

> When the wind is in the east
> It's neither fit for man nor beast.

'I never heard that before, and I don't
think it is pretty,' retorted Léonie.

'Not pretty but forcible.   The terms are
hardly synonymous.'   Quentin broke off in
his remark and dragged down a bunch of
scarlet berries adorning the hedge beside
them.   'This speaks of winter,' he said,
putting it into his companion's hand.   'Oh,
but I forgot you don't know what an English
winter is yet.'

'I know it is jolly cold,' returned the girl
absently.

Lee put up his hand scandalised.

'You must not say "jolly cold,"' he re-
monstrated.   'It is a slang expression.'

'But you used it just a little while ago.'

'Possibly—but then I am a man.'

'And because I am a woman I must be
restricted to yes and no, charmingly fine,

exceedingly cold?' said Léonie, whose six months' life in England had so familiarised her with the language, that she was no longer guilty of the extraordinary arrangement of words and sentences which had so distracted Connisterre in his desire to pass her off as 'not a foreigner at all.'

'My dear girl, you don't expect to use quite the same expressions as escape my lips sometimes?'

'But why not. When are you going back to London, Mr. Lee?'

'That is rather a painful question. Your tone suggests that it would be an infinite relief for you to know that an actual period is fixed to my sojourn in Forest Deane.'

'Oh dear no! I like you being here, for it is a change from the quiet. Ah, *ciel!*' shrugging her shoulders, as she stripped off a twig of the red berries and put it in the breast of her dark gray coat. 'Your England it is very dull, very *triste;* your skies never smile, as do the skies abroad;

they weep, weep, weep always, and here it
is dreadful. I wish I could run away. What
is London like? I mean, what is it to live
in London?'

'Infernally dull sometimes. One long
grind, and slave, and grind, fooling round in
an office trying to make money, and always
failing.'

'But every one must work.'

'True, oh most juvenile mentor! but some
people like it less than others, don't you see?
Even Connisterre plodding along through
oils, and turpentine, and paints, grows as dull
and as sticky as his own brushes sometimes.
Still he's one of the hard-working sort, is
Connisterre, and what is more, one of the
successful ones too.'

'Ah, and you live with him now,' said
Léonie, growing suddenly interested. 'Why
do you?'

Quentin laughed.

'He made me. He said, "Look here,
old man, you'll go to ruin with the speed of

a switchback if there is nobody at hand to pull you up. Pack your traps and bring them round to my place. The old house is big enough to hold us both, and I ought not to forget that I have £250 locked up in you. It behoves me as a careful man to keep watch over my receipt "—meaning me,' added Quentin, tapping his chest. 'So I went. He is a good sort is the dear old man, only as the Scotch say, "gey quick wi' his temper."'

'But I don't quite understand what you mean,' said Léonie, in some perplexity. 'I thought receipts were little bits of paper which people put on a file.'

Lee threw back his head and laughed aloud.

'Exactly; I am the bit of paper, don't you see, and Connisterre—well Connisterre is the file. He lent me money once when I was up a tree, and so far I haven't been able to pay it all back. May Providence hasten the day,' he added, piously. 'My soul abhors economy.'

'But what tree? why did you want money there?' persisted Léonie, whose English vocabulary, although an extensive one, by no means included all Mr. Quentin Lee's slang expressions.

'Up a tree? Why, in queer street, in a hole, a tight place, a distracting fix—oh, don't you see,' as Léonie only looked more and more bewildered. 'Well, in plain English, since abstruse is no use to you, I was in a mess, and wanted money which Connisterre very generously forked out—I mean lent to me, upon the understanding that I must pay it back when convenient. Upon my soul,' Lee wiped his heated face, 'if one's native tongue is not as difficult to speak sometimes as double Dutch! Do you understand now mademoiselle?'

'Madame,' corrected the girl in a little dignified manner infinitely amusing to Lee, who could never bring himself to look upon Léonie as other than a child. 'Of course I understand now, but why do you use such

queer words, why did you not say at once
that you were in debt, that is the expression
is it not? It is foolish to have so many
words to mean the same thing. Are there
many more?'

'Yes, all those which I ran through just
now and half a hundred besides. I think I
must take your education in hand mademoiselle—madame, I mean. You can express
yourself more forcibly in slang.'

'Slang? What is slang?

'The emphatic language of the child of
nature,' returned Lee with apparent gravity.
'When you use slang, you express your
meaning in bold and inelegant words; on
the other hand, when you use what is termed
"elegant English," you gain in polish what
you lose in brevity. Now, for instance, if
you had been riding at a rapid pace, the
slang vocabulary would teach you to describe
it something like this. "We had a rattling
good spin over the field, and, by Jove, didn't
I make the brute show a clean pair of heels!"'

'And in English it would be—— ? '

'My horse carried me in an exceedingly rapid and satisfactory manner over the field. His rate of speed left nothing to be desired.'

'Then a rattling good spin is the same as a gallop,' said Léonie, knitting her brows thoughtfully. 'I must remember that. A rattling good—did you say spin ? I thought to spin was to use that funny little old wheel which stands in the hall. People used to make wool for stockings on it, I know—at least somebody told me so.'

'I don't know much about stockings except that they have a nasty habit of coming in holes after twelve hours' wear,' said Quentin frankly. 'It is almost better to go barefoot —Highland fashion.

'Highland, that is in Scotland is it not? We were to have gone there this autumn, but——'

'It did not come off.'

'What come off? '

'The tour. Your plans suffered a material

alteration, thereby causing you to remain in England. I have put that neatly anyway,' added Lee.

'But these Highland men. They wear stockings?'

'Highlanders we say.'

'Well Highlanders then.'

'No they don't wear stockings.'

'How do they dress?'

'Oh in a sort of short toga—Roman fashion,' said Lee, with a twinkle in his eye. 'They wear a petticoat and a three-cornered cap, and carry a sort of kangaroo pouch to hold their dagger and their bawbees.'

'I don't believe you,' returned Léonie crushingly; and Lee shouted until the woods rang again.

'But it is true for all that,' he said when he had recovered himself. 'Is not the vicar coming in this afternoon? Suppose you ask him if the Highlanders don't wear just what I have said. I bet you a pony, if you like, he says yes.'

'But I shall not be allowed to keep the pony if I win it,' she said disconsolately. 'Lady Paget does not approve of my riding.'

'Oh you literal young person,' groaned Quentin. 'I don't mean a four-legged quadruped. Look here, mademoiselle, otherwise madame, otherwise Mrs. Connisterre, I certainly will draw up a dictionary of selected terms in alphabetical order, so that when you are not quite sure of a term you may consult it.'

'But I do not hear others speak as you do,' she objected.

'They are not so well educated perhaps.'

Quentin Lee's eyes were brimming over with fun. He was young enough and mischievous enough to enjoy training this little brown-eyed witch in the way she should *not* go. He had heard a great deal about her from Connisterre who, at the time Léonie came under Lady Paget's guardianship, was unaware that lady possessed the somewhat doubtful privilege of owning Mr. Quentin Lee

as a nephew.   It was with no little surprise
that Geoffrey learned, from an accidental remark after Lee took up residence with him,
of this connection with Lady Paget.   At
present Quentin was spending a few days
with Lady Paget in her Derbyshire home,
and consequently saw a great deal of Léonie
in what she was wont to term her off-duty
time.   He was wonderfully bright and genial,
full of good nature and high spirits, which at
times ran away with him altogether, and his
coming had been like a ray of sunshine across
the girl's quiet life.   He was a link, too, between herself and Connisterre.   She had seen
nothing of the latter since they parted nearly
five months ago in Genoa, but she entertained for him a romantic devotion and gratitude which Geoffrey had very wisely decided
to check in the bud.   He had lost a good deal
already through this act of quixotic chivalry,
and he was by no means minded to add to
his perplexities by assuming the sole control
of Léonie's future.   It was better, he argued

to himself, when the softer side of his nature cried out against leaving her so entirely amongst strangers to a life whose conventional decorum must war against every instinct of her Bohemian nature—better that she should learn to accept her position at once and depend upon herself, than assume that he would be always at her beck and call and a constant referee in the little trials of temper, despair, and loneliness which must inevitably ensue. There had been, however, something in Léonie's big brown eyes when he left her at Genoa with Lady Paget, which haunted him unpleasantly, something of the mute anguish and entreaty which had looked out at him from the liquid orbs of a favourite old dog whom he had reluctantly ordered to be destroyed some years before. He remembered how the bright light faded from Saladin's eyes, drowned in a mist of actual tears, remembered the dash forward as he had left the room, the howl of entreaty which had never before been left unanswered, and insensibly the little affair

connected itself with Léonie.   In justice to
her and to himself, he had left her to fight
the battle alone, acting no doubt wisely
by so doing, but Leonié, who knew nothing
of his motives, thought him just a little
unkind.

When she spoke again after Lee's frivolous
remarks concerning Highlanders, it was with
a change of subject and some resentment in
her tone.

' I wonder will Mr. Connisterre ever come
to see me here.'

'Some day, perhaps.   When he is taking
his Christmas holidays he might drop down
for a day or two just to see that you are
keeping out of mischief.'

' Did he say so ? '

' I never heard him, but he might.   Look
here, I'll have you a race to the gate which
leads into the garden.   Now, start fair.'

'But you ought to give me half a dozen
yards.'

'Not a bit of it when I have a gun to

carry—well, perhaps, three yards; now, one, two, three—off.'

Suiting action to the word, away went the fleet young figures through the gathering shadows, scampering with easy celerity over the thick undergrowth of brush and bramble, or tripping ever so slightly on the interlaced leaves of the golden bracken. Undignified perhaps? Well yes, I daresay, but who can deny the pleasure of a race through some forest on a bright sharp autumn evening, a race which brings the blood surging warmly through one's veins, a race with the fresh cold air cutting like an icy breath across one's face, and the yellow leaves whirling by hundreds overhead? Léonie's cheeks were glowing like two June roses when, a loser by a couple of lengths, she came at last to a full stop in view of a gate which led into the manor garden, and leaned laughing and out of breath against the gnarled trunk of an old oak which reared its lofty head skyward like a very Titan amongst its fellows.

'You are too quick for me,' she panted, stooping to recover a truant hair-pin which had fallen amongst the russet leaves at her feet. 'I cannot run so fast.'

'You mended your pace towards the last though. A sort of final spurt, but you have not learned how to get your second wind or keep your elbows in. Still it is fair running for a girl even if you are a bit pumped. Shall we have another back again.'

'No thank you,' she laughed. 'We shall be seen by some one. You do tempt me to go wrong, Mr. Lee.'

'I am very sorry.' Quentin leaned his arms upon the low gate. They were within a stone's throw of the house now but it was impossible to proceed until Léonie had re-gained her breath. It was quiet as death out there under the giant trees, with no sight or sound of life about them now that the birds and scampering rabbits had gone to sleep. The house, long, low, and old-fashioned, had modern French windows opening out into the terraced garden; these were an innovation of Lady Paget's—one of the few, very few instances during her married life in which her wishes had been yielded to, and were in consequence a source of perpetual irritation to Sir John. A perfect wealth of Virginia creeper covered the front of the house from roof to basement, crimson now as a robin's breast. An open porch, reached by three shallow steps, and supported by slender pillars, formed the main entrance, and from this, depending like a scarlet curtain of leaves, the creeper afforded a partial shelter from the breeze. The tennis ground, a little short of full size and rarely used, ran along one end of the house, and a small conservatory jutting out from the drawing-room faced it across the bed of turf which separated them. There was an air of rigid propriety and peace about the whole aspect of Manor House, or the Hall as it had been formerly called. Nothing wild nor picturesque nor romantic in its surroundings save where, right away in the distance, the wild Derbyshire hills, with all their stores of legendary lore, flanked one another in successive heights of blue and purple.   From where these two truants were standing, they could see into the drawing-room, a recently-lighted lamp revealing the inmates with bright distinctness.   Its glow threw into bold relief the figure of a man in clerical attire, whose strongly marked features were noticeable even at this distance.   There were two other people in the room, an elderly lady in a white cap and shawl knitting by the fire, and a younger one, sharper featured, trim, grave, and observant.   This was Monica Paget and Léonie's *bête noire*.   It was hardly to be wondered at that the conventional propriety of the one should war against the Bohemian lawlessness of the other, and many were the skirmishes, open and concealed, between these two very dissimilar people.

'Now is your chance to ask about the Highland petticoat,' said Lee, holding open the gate for Léonie to pass through.   'The reverend gentleman ought surely to know. He is of Scotch extraction, and I daresay wears a kilt when on his native heath. Ah, the curtain falls; interval of ten minutes between this and the next act.'

Taking advantage of the housemaid having come forward to draw the blinds, Léonie fled away across the grass with the speed of a lapwing, and disappeared within the creeper-covered porch, leaving Quentin Lee to follow more slowly.

CHAPTER XIII

GOOD NEWS

Be well aware, quoth then that lady mild,
Lest sudden mischief ye too rash provoke.

SPENSER.

FIVE minutes later Léonie entered the drawing-room, a deep tinge in her usually pale
cheeks testifying to the recent ramble. Lady
Paget greeted her with a pleasant smile,
Monica with the shadow of a frown.

'I wish you would choose some other time
in the day for your walk than this,' she said
in a low tone as the girl, having shaken
hands with the rector, came towards the little
tea table where Monica was sitting. 'You
know that I wish you to be always in at five
to relieve me from attending to the tea.'

Léonie bit her lip. The colour had

warmed to a deep crimson on her cheeks, more at Miss Paget's tone than the actual words. Of course she should have been in. None knew that better than Léonie herself.

'I did not know it was so late,' she replied. Quentin, who had overheard his cousin's remark, wisely repressed a retort.

'You have a watch?'

'Yes.'

'Then for the future see that it corresponds with the drawing-room clock.'

This time Léonie did not speak. She knew she was in the wrong, and for a wonder kept her temper. Certain duties fell to her share which were not sufficiently onerous or extensive to excuse her omitting any of them, but Miss Paget's manner of recalling one to a sense of shortcoming was distinctly unpleasant, and almost always roused what was worst in Léonie's nature. Lady Paget, placid, meek, and weak-willed, was content to allow most of the household

management to slip into her daughter's hands,
but occasionally she would interfere upon
Léonie's behalf, giving her unexpected little
pleasures, or shielding her from Monica's re-
proof.   The girl filled an anomalous position
which it was not easy to define, combining a
sort of dual companionship to mother and
daughter, the latter of whom was a staunch
church worker, and head of nobody could
count how many committees, unions, classes,
and guilds.   Léonie used to wonder a little
wearily sometimes why Miss Paget could not
distribute more charity at home and less
abroad.   She disliked Monica almost as
much as she disliked Sir John himself,
who bullied his household impartially, from
his wife down to the smallest hireling upon
the premises.

'You were not at our *conversazione* last
night,' said the rector, turning round and
affably addressing Léonie, who had seated
herself by Lady Paget, and was picking
up some dropped stitches in the old

lady's knitting. 'I understood you were coming.'

'I asked if I might be excused,' replied the girl frankly, raising her eyes to Mr. Taylor's clever face. 'I did not enjoy the last. It was so very dull that I felt *triste* for a week after.'

The rector looked nonplussed. These *conversazioni* were a pet project of his own. Monica's face grew a shade colder.

'But there were a great many people there,' he demurred after a short pause. 'They appeared to enjoy it.'

Léonie shrugged her shoulders.

'I did not,' she said, her little gipsy face full of mischief.' We went in like—like a flock of sheep, spoke to—no, I did not speak to any one, I think. I sat on a chair near some palms which kept tickling my neck most unpleasantly, and then sometimes we went to the tables to look at pictures and old books. I did not like them, but they were valuable. They had some—do you call it cut woods in ? '

' No, woodcuts.'

' Ah, well it is all the same. Then there was some music and two little songs. I did not mind the songs, only they were not so lively as those you sing, Mr. Lee. I mean that one about a bicycle—— '

' A bicycle built for two ?' said Lee gravely.

' Yes, and what is the other. Down by the old Suan—— something river. I don't quite remember. Then there was a recitation in very bad French, and some more looking at books, after which we came away. I did not like to go to another, Mr. Taylor.'

The rector's impassive face relaxed into a smile.

' You are candid, at all events,' he said, putting down his cup.

' Don't you think, Léonie, that it is rather bad taste to satirise the efforts of others who are exerting themselves to give pleasure ?

If you are too clever to enjoy it, at least say nothing in depreciation,' remarked Miss Paget frigidly.

'But I meant not to be rude,' returned Léonie plaintively.' Mr. Taylor asked why I did not go, so I told him. Why should one permit one's self to be bored?'

'Ah why indeed,' said Quentin, slowly stirring his tea. 'There is only this, mademoiselle, if some of us did not permit ourselves to be bored society would be in a state of incandescent war. Two-thirds of the people with whom one meets have no other object in life than to bore the remaining third, and the question arises whether passive boredom or active defiance is the most wearying to the system. It is a monotonous place the world.'

'Youth and pessimism do not go well together, Mr. Lee,' said the rector rather stiffly. 'It has become fashionable to rail at society and the hollowness of the world, but we do expect the privilege, if indeed it is one, to be assumed only by those who have lived long enough to prove that human nature is often disappointing. If you are a pessimist at twenty, you will be an atheist at thirty, which God forbid.'

'I am neither one nor the other at present,' retorted Lee equably. 'There are worse evils than being bored, but I may never reach them. Indeed for anything I know or care, Bellamy's Utopia may yet come to pass, and give us all a three years' or more menial training. I daresay it would be a good thing.'

'You refer to his *Looking Backward?* That is a far-fetched idea, but the working-classes, socialistic and otherwise, seem to have a craze for it. Mr. Oliver Meredith and I were discussing the pernicious effect of such a book yesterday.'

'Meredith? Let me see, do I know him?'

'You know his brother-in-law, Mr Carter,' said Monica, picking up her work.

'Is that insufferable puppy his brother-in-law? Well, I wish him joy. If there is one man I cannot stand it is that Carter,' returned Lee.

'Simply on the ground that his father was a retail tradesman I suppose,' said the rector, who for some reason or other seemed inclined to have his knife into Quentin Lee this afternoon.

'I hope I am not quite such a snob,' returned the other warmly. 'I don't care a cent what a person does to earn his own living, provided he puts his best energies into it, and takes a pride in his work. I have the very greatest respect for any one who has the capability to rise from the ranks by his own hard labour. For what does it signify whether you are a doctor or a sweep, so long as you work to the best of your ability? It is when I see a man like that Carter giving himself the airs of a grand duke, behaving as if he had been born in the purple, looking down with lofty contempt upon men who are in trade, while every one knows that his own father made money in business, and that he

himself not so long ago was at the beck and
call of a customer, that I have a contempt for
him. I wonder he isn't ashamed of his paltry
pride. Does he suppose other people go
about with their eyes closed, that he hides
his head like an ostrich in the sand ; besides,
he puts a premium on ill-natured remarks.
Nobody, unless he were an arrant snob,
would cast it up against Carter as something
of which to be ashamed, that his father made
money by keeping a shop ; but when as I
say, he gives himself the airs of a grand
duke, then the world, quite as well informed
as himself, is always ready to pull him down
from such a contemptible pedestal.'

' I admit all you say, but the man is rather
to be pitied that he cannot get over his false
pride,' said the rector.'

' Pity ? I don't pity him or any other
such insufferable puppy. He comes of a
trading family, and why can't he admit it ?
Every one respected and admired the old
man.'

'You are not in trade, Mr. Lee?'

'No I am not.'

'Nor was your father?'

'No, nor my grandfather, nor even further still, but there is no particular merit in the fact. It is simply an accident of birth, and I don't assume airs in consequence. I like to choose my friends for what they are, and not for what they do. I am sure I have known quite as great cads amongst professional men as business men.'

'You are a sad radical, Quentin,' said Lady Paget shaking her head.

'On the contrary, I have no political views,' he returned laughing. 'If my sentiments are radical, well, they must be so, they are at least natural.'

The arrival of the afternoon post effected a diversion. With a word of apology, Lady Paget opened a letter bearing the London post-mark, and gave a little pleasurable exclamation.

Monica looked up.

'It is from Geoffrey Connisterre,' said her mother, passing the letter across. 'If he can arrange, he is coming here to-morrow for one night on his way north.'

'Oh!' exclaimed Léonie, jumping up with the impetuous delight of a child, while the book on her knee fell with a noisy clatter to the floor. 'You mean he is coming here, here! How delightful, madame. You will ask him to stay a very long time, will you not? Oh, I shall be *so* glad to see him.'

Had a thunderbolt fallen into the centre of Lady Paget's drawing-room, it could hardly have produced more consternation than did Léonie's outburst of unconventional delight as she looked from one to another of the little party for sympathy in her joy.

'Now you have put your foot into it,' murmured Quentin to himself, as he stooped for the fallen book.

'Really, Léonie,' began Miss Paget in a voice portentous of the coming storm, while

Lady Paget, with a stiffness unusual to her, remarked—

'It is not customary in England to speak so extravagantly about the visit of a friend. I am glad to see that you are not unmindful of Mr. Connisterre's kindness, but it would be as well to remember that he is after all only a chance acquaintance, and will neither expect nor like such demonstrative gratitude.'

The rebuke was delivered in so low a tone as to be inaudible to other than Léonie, but Mr. Taylor, who guessed at the girl's embarrassment, created a diversion in her favour by an abrupt change of subject, and the little passage of arms came to a temporary stop.

CHAPTER XIV

A TROUBLESOME CHARGE

My fate doth grow
So luckless now
That—do you know
Beyond all telling
My life I hate ;
Thus desperate,
In woeful state
   I still am dwelling.

CHAUCER.

LÉONIE awakened the following morning with a thrill of pleasurable expectation warming every fibre of her being. The lecture upon the impropriety of her conduct the preceding evening had fallen very lightly upon her conscience. Miss Paget could not take away the pleasure which Geoffrey Connisterre's visit would bring, could not prevent her seeing him ; besides, who knew, he might have news of Gerard, and life with Gerard, providing it were spent in the sunny lands of France or Italy, would be preferable to this monotonous existence, even if she had to sacrifice her pride to obtain it. And yet it was very beautiful here in England sometimes, thought Léonie, when she flung open her bedroom window and leaned out to inhale the fresh sweet morning air. It was an unusually bright October day, fair and sunshiny, with just a touch of frost beautifying the country side. The short grass below her window shone and sparkled like a thousand diamonds in the early sun ; every little twig and every russet leaf had its powdery coat of white also. Dame Frost was laying an early touch upon the autumn foliage. Away in the distance a blue haze lay lovingly over the giant hills and peaceful low-lying valleys, a haze through which the bright rays of the sun cut sharply like a scythe, piling it up in prodigal heaps on the mountain sides and rambling country lanes. By and by a sharp

wind might creep up to complete the work,
and, scattering the misty curtains, would reveal the world in all its clear gay beauty.
Léonie leaned out a little further. From her
point of vantage she could see a silver streak
winding its way through a distant meadow
towards the copse where she and Quentin
Lee had been the preceding evening. This
was a tiny arm of the Trent, and for long
after Léonie's arrival at Forest Deane had
provided her with amusement watching the
spreckled trout diving to and fro amongst
the stones, their movements distinctly visible
in the clear water. The birds were calling
to one another from tree to tree, grumbling
perhaps at this early approach of winter,
while Madoc, the curly-haired spaniel, was
lying upon the grass, burrowing excitedly for
some hidden treasure. He looked up at
Léonie's call, wagged a shaggy tail in response, then set to work once more upon
his researches. Time just then was
precious to Madoc, and retribution in the

shape of a gardener might wait upon his steps.

'Madoc, Madoc, mon cher, que cherchez-vous?' cried the girl, flinging her straw hat down upon his back, which glinted like satin in the sunshine. 'Vous êtes un méchant chien. Voyez, ce que vous avez fait dans le——' But at this moment Miss Paget, armed with a huge pair of scissors and a watering can, made her appearance from the conservatory. Léonie, guessing that a conversation carried on between herself and Madoc at the distance which separated them would be unpleasing to Miss Paget, drew in her head with some rapidity, but the retreat was too late. A reprimand followed later on.

'Léonie, I wish you would cease this unladylike habit of flinging open your window and calling to the dog,' Miss Paget said as they sat down to the breakfast table. 'And also will you kindly remember to speak English. You are as yet so very far from perfect in the language that I think it shows a great lack of perseverance to refrain from speaking it at every possible opportunity.' This was rather unjust to Léonie, who both spoke and read English with unusual ease for a girl who had spent all her life on the Continent.

'But, indeed, I can speak English very well,' she said, helping herself to marmalade. 'There is nothing I have to learn except some slang.'

Quentin gave her a warning look, but she proceeded undeterred.

'Mr. Lee says that slang is so much more forcible than elegant English. Do you know all the slang, Miss Paget?'

'I am happy to say that I do not know any,' returned Monica stiffly.

'Oh, come now, Monica, that is not true,' put in Quentin, who stood in no awe of his cousin, and rather delighted in trampling upon her pet prejudices. 'You were not always cut and dried into flannel petticoats and district work. If you would only get rid of this rabid curatical mania,—curatical, there is a good term for you, Mademoiselle Léonie, —you would be as much a brick of a girl as you were formerly.'

It was impossible to suppress Quentin ; Monica dropped the subject.

'What time is Connisterre expected to arrive,' asked the young scapegrace after a short pause. His eyes were twinkling with amusement at having, as he would express it, scored off his cousin. 'I might take the dog-cart down to meet him if you are engaged, Monica ?'

Léonie opened her lips as if about to speak, finally thought better of it, and said nothing.

'I think the train is 5.15. Yes, you may have the dogcart, Quentin. I am going out this afternoon, but I expect to be home before six, and probably Mr. Connisterre will excuse my not being here to meet him.'

There was mute entreaty in Léonie's big brown eyes as she looked across the table at

Quentin Lee, a request which she did not dare to put into words ; but whatever hopes had risen to her heart by reason of Miss Paget's absence from home during the afternoon, were dashed a moment later to the ground.

' Léonie you must arrange the flowers and finish what work you have in hand early this morning,' proceeded Miss Paget tranquilly. ' I wish you to help me with the cutting out at the sewing class this afternoon, and later on go to the rectory for an hour or two. I promised Mrs. Taylor you should assist her with those children's pinafores for the Christmas treat, and she suggested this evening as being the most convenient to her. You can go straight on from the schoolroom, and I will send Dobson for you about nine or half-past.'

For one brief moment Léonie meditated open defiance, meditated perhaps hurling her plate to the ground like some spoilt child denied what it ardently covets. But rebellion was useless. There could be no appeal against

Miss Paget's commands. Léonie remained silent, but there was a flash of the bright eyes, a mutinous quiver of the red lips which spoke something of the torrent of anger within. She knew from woeful experience what was meant by this long evening spent at the rectory; an interminable stitch, stitch, stitch at those abominable print pinafores, a patient listening to the insipid conversation of the rector's wife, a vain effort to concentrate her attention and interest upon the details of chicken pox, whooping cough, and the like, just then devastating the parish. And then to think what she would be losing through this enforced evening at the rectory—Mr. Connisterre's society, the bright change which his advent would bring, the pleasure of seeing him again. His visit, too, would be so short. Oh, it was hard, very hard. No wonder Léonie's face grew like a thunder cloud, but it was out of her power to object. Did these people not pay her thirty pounds a year to minister to their wants?

Human nature which does not require a *quid pro quo* is hardly human nature at all. Miss Paget exacted hers to the uttermost farthing ; and the fact of Léonie not wishing to sew pinafores that evening did not weigh with her in the least. Why should it? Léonie was not engaged to entertain Mr. Connisterre or any other of the Manor House guests. Perhaps the girl might consider herself in some measure as interested in this particular one, but now that she had virtually left his protection for another far more suitable, it was in the interests of propriety better that they should be kept apart.

'Am I to remain, then, the whole evening at the rectory?' asked Léonie, lifting her eyes for one moment to Miss Paget's.

'It is of little use going for a shorter time. Dobson shall come for you.'

'I think I can bring myself home in safety without the aid of Dobson,' said the girl rather disdainfully. 'It is only a hundred yards away.'

'It is exactly one mile, and you will wait there until Dobson comes. I do not choose to allow either you or any other young girl to wander alone about the lanes at night.' Miss Paget was apt to overlook the fact that Léonie, child though she might be, was a married woman, and as such might have been entitled to a little more liberty. Indeed, it may be questioned whether anybody in the Manor House ever remembered the fact at all.

Vanquished, but by no means resigned, Léonie dropped the subject. Quentin Lee, not deceived by this apparent acquiescence, watched her in some amusement and with a great deal of sympathy also. He was sorry for her, but to interfere on her behalf was futile and would only make matters worse. Léonie looked after him enviously when later on he picked up the *Times* and retired to the low window seat to read in comfort. Once it had been her happy lot to possess such freedom; to take the *Figaro* and skim its contents in lazy comfort. Now it was all so different. In place of the idle lounge, the canaries were to feed, the poodle to exercise, the flowers to trim, the parish pinafores to sew. Trifles no doubt in themselves, but oh, what a hideous knack have women's trifles of piling themselves into one large ball under which the feminine Sisyphus must stagger up the hill.

'It is very nice to be you with nothing to do but amuse yourself,' she said resentfully to Quentin, when the course of her morning's occupations brought him under her notice.

'It is, indeed, most sapient counsellor,' he rejoined, puffing lazily at a cigarette while he watched her rearranging a bowl of flowers amongst a mass of Virginia creeper which she had culled for a background to the yellow blossoms. 'There are two luxuries in this life, saith a philosopher. The luxury of working, and the luxury of watching others work. I myself prefer the passive to the active form. There is in it a sense of reflected labour which is infinitely more restful than the actual fact. Life, as our esteemed friend, —was his name Mantanelli?—remarked, "is one long demnition grind."'

'What is a demnition grind?' asked Léonie, glancing up from her work.

'It is not a pretty expression for a young lady. I do not think the reverend Augustus would approve of your choice of language.'

'It was not mine—you used it.'

'So I did, so I did, little wiseacre.' Lee got up with an effort, and propped his broad shoulders against the window.

'I am growing disgracefully stout,' he said, regarding his stalwart limbs pensively. 'Twelve stone if an ounce. I must train, or the football season will knock me out of time.'

'Train? oh, that means to grow thinner, so that you can walk about? The curate, Mr. Sylvester, said to me a day or two ago that

he must go into training. I could not think
at first what he meant.'

'*He* train,' said Lee scornfully. 'His idea
of training stops at a cold bath and keeping
his bedroom window open half an inch at
night. Bless me, he couldn't stand a genuine
train, that baby. He would be as thin as a
sixpence and as limp as a jelly-fish in a
week. Look here, mademoiselle, are you
going to play truant this afternoon, and
come with me to meet Connisterre? Never
mind the flannel petticoats—upon my soul, the
old pauper women of England might wear
nothing but flannel petticoats, considering
the time which is devoted to making those
wonderful garments by curate-bitten damsels.
You steal away. It will be a lovely drive,'
but Léonie, who had still a conscience left,
put her hands over her ears and ran away to
exercise the poodle, who was full of years and
scant of breath.

'Poor little beggar,' said Quentin com-
miseratingly. 'I thank my stars I'm not a

girl,' he added a moment after, thus putting into words the voiceless pæan of thanksgiving which rises more or less fervently in the hearts of all men. 'Grinding in an office for the almighty dollar may have its disadvantages, but it is a deuced sight more exciting than walking out the poodle, or driving out in a brougham with both the windows closed and smothered in a fur rug.'

These reflections occurred to him again later on in the day when he was driving Connisterre through Forest Deane in the dogcart. It was a sharp evening, sharp almost to bitterness, for the wind had risen and was singing a croony sort of melody above them in the trees. Now and again a passing shower of rain, wetting and unpleasant, came drip, drip on to the carpet of leaves lining the county lane, reducing it to a sodden pulpy mass very different from its former crispness. To the two men wrapped up in overcoats and sheltered by a rug, the inclemency of the afternoon was nothing.

Indeed, Connisterre, after his long warm journey, rather revelled in the biting force of the wind.

'It is a lonely bit of country this,' he said, puffing at a cigar as his eyes roamed over the spreading fields and the dusky mountains beyond. 'I like it well enough in the summer, but, by Jove, in winter the wind does sweep round here. Has that mare cast a shoe, Lee? She stumbles.'

'Not a bit of it—the old humbug. I understand her little tricks. She is full of idleness and oats, and raises as much fuss over a hill the size of a walnut as an old maid would over a stolen kiss. There now, I told you it was all laziness,' as at a sharp cut of the whip the indignant mare plunged forward and fled along the road at a rapid pace, 'just the wiles of her sex, but she doesn't take me in.'

'You seem to have formed an adverse opinion of womenkind at an early age,' said Connisterre, lighting another cigar. 'Do

you base your conclusions on'—puff—'the
fact that'—puff—'they possess so ——
Hang the thing! Give me a match,
Quentin. This fool of a cigar won't draw.'

'I base it upon personal experience only.
You don't know a woman if you live a
hundred and fifty years with her,' returned
Lee, handing over his match-box, a very
chaste affair, with Q. L. engraved on one
side. 'Don't drop that, please; it was a
present. How have you been getting along
without me all this time? You missed the
fillip of my society, I suppose, as you are
looking me up here.'

'Not quite that. I wished to see the
Pagets and my small charge before I went
north for a fortnight's shooting.'

'When are you coming back to London?'

'Not until the middle or end of January.
I suppose you can get along without me,'
Geoffrey added, laying his hand on Lee's arm.

There was some meaning in his tone.
Quentin reddened.

' I should be a beast if I couldn't,' he said
energetically ; then in a lower tone : 'What
you have been to me, Connisterre! what you
have saved me from ! '

They were silent. It was only in brief
moments like this that Connisterre realised
how great an influence he had gained over
Quentin Lee. He was thankful, and yet it
humbled him. There were pages in his own
life which he scarcely dared to turn. Were
they quite fitting ones for a self-constituted
mentor to possess ? '

' You have seen a good deal of my protégée,
I suppose,' he went on after the short pause.

' I see that she gets well bullied,' returned
Lee frankly.

' What do you mean ? '

' Just what I say. *I* call it bullying.
They don't, of course, starve or otherwise
maltreat her, but she is not the sort of girl to
run well in the harness you have put upon
her, my dear fellow. Little things which a
more phlegmatic temperament would never

notice but simply absorb like a sponge, drive her distracted. She cannot settle down into the mindless, nerveless ideal sort of companion necessary for this place.'

'Suppose you explain what you mean,' said Connisterre rather coldly, manlike resenting the impeachment that his judgment had been at fault. 'If you or Léonie expect to find any subordinate position—no matter what it may be—all honey and sweetness, you will very soon find out your mistake.'

'Oh, she does not complain to me, but I can see as far through a brick wall as most people. She is not happy, bless her little soul, how could she be under these circumstances? You know what the coachman said to his mistress: "It isn't 'opping over the 'igh 'edges as 'urts the 'orse's 'oofs, but it's the 'ammer, 'ammer, 'ammer on the 'ard 'igh road as does it." So it is the 'ammer, 'ammer, 'ammer on the 'ard 'igh road of daily routine which wears out Mademoiselle Léonie's patience at present.'

Connisterre laughed, but he still looked rather annoyed.

'They keep nagging at her, or rather Monica does all day. I wonder what some people's Christianity is worth! The poor child was wild with delight at the thought of you coming to-day, and if she did express herself a little more fervently than is considered good taste by the cut-and-dried laws of conventional society, what did it signify? However, Monica has carried her off an unwilling victim to the Juggernaut car of parish work and such like rubbish. You will not see her to-night.'

'I shall see her in the morning, then,' said Connisterre outwardly unmoved, but inwardly indignant at the story. 'A little wholesome discipline will be good for her. She is an emotional, highly-strung sort of child, and probably exaggerates her troubles. I must talk it over and see if they cannot be made easier, but one feels afraid to advise.'

'For my part, I think it is easier to advise

than act,' said Lee, whipping up the mare again. 'Any one can say what *ought* to be done, the difficulty lies in the *doing*. Here we are.'

Connisterre's welcome was a warm one. Apart from her wish to bring about a match between himself and Monica, Lady Paget had a genuine liking for the artist. It was solely in order to please him that she had consented to receive Léonie into her house, setting aside some natural misgivings as to the result, but the experiment had not worked so badly as might have been feared. There was friction between the girl and Monica, friction which often ended unpleasantly, but Lady Paget never troubled over trifles. She found Léonie attentive, good natured, and amusing, and what was more important still, Sir John, who usually growled at any new member of the household, had chosen through some freak or other to tolerate her presence with equanimity. Léonie stood in no awe of the baronet. She even dared contradict him openly and stand up for herself when attacked, so that, taking all things into consideration, Lady Paget had not, so far, regretted her act of good nature.

' I hope you have found my little protégée useful,' Connisterre remarked, after dinner, when he had skilfully brought the conversation round to Léonie. ' I thought that after her strangeness had worn off she would prove rather a pleasant addition to your family.'

' So she has,' said Lady Paget placidly ; ' she is very bright and cheerful. A little wilful, perhaps, but time will alter that.'

' If we required any one with much ability or talent, I think we should have to look elsewhere for her,' remarked Miss Paget, cutting an end of silk from her work with a decided snap. ' Léonie is really—we call her Léonie, it seemed so absurd to address her as Mrs. Connisterre, your own name too —Léonie is lamentably ignorant.'

'Is she?' Connisterre pulled his moustache, and looked across at Monica.

'Most ignorant, and has no desire to improve herself. I suggested her taking a course of painting lessons, but she refused quite brusquely, saying that any attempts of hers would be an insult to nature; she could not sketch a Cochin China hen correctly. This is a sample of the odd remarks she utters sometimes. She makes me quite nervous when strangers are visiting us. Quite recently, when the dear bishop was over for a confirmation service, and dined here, she asked him the most idiotic and leading questions with reference to ballet girls and stage life. I was quite embarrassed, and naturally it makes people wonder who or what she is.'

'He professed ignorance, of course,' said Connisterre, rather amused by Léonie's vagaries; while Quentin Lee laughed outright.'

Miss Paget frowned.

'Then you do not think that she is quite suitable for a companion?' went on Geoffrey, looking rather perturbed.

'She may improve, and in the meantime her duties here are so light that it does not require much capability to perform them. It is better she should be in safe surroundings, rather than exposed to the temptations of a town; and if this calls for some measure of self-sacrifice upon our part, we ought not to grudge it.'

Connisterre began to wonder whether Léonie were not, after all, much to be pitied; whether a quiet home, plenty of food, ortho-dox surroundings, were calculated to satisfy all the wants of this vagrant little soul.

'I am sure I am very much obliged to you,' he began lamely. 'I feel in a measure responsible for her welfare and happiness, you see.'

'You are an unsuitable person to take the responsibility of such a charge,' growled Sir John, whom an incipient attack of gout had rendered more quarrelsome than usual. 'In my young days it was the grandmothers and aunts who were supposed to look after giddy girls, not bachelors of eight-and-twenty. Now then, idiot!' This to the footman, who was in the room replenishing the fire, and in so doing had the misfortune to upset the poker, which fell down with a noisy clatter into the hearth. 'It beats creation you cannot see to a fire without all this infernal noise. If it occurs again you may leave—you may leave; do you understand?'

Thomas, who was new to the house, turned scarlet, and left the room with some precipitation. Familiarity had not yet inured him to the violence of Sir John's temper.

'Lor, that's a trifle,' said the butler, when Thomas inveighed against the injustice. 'He'd make nothin' of flingin' the poker at your head if he was so inclined.'

'There goes a born fool, if ever there was one in this world,' growled Sir John, as the door closed upon the unfortunate menial.

'Susan, if you cannot find more efficient servants you had better give up housekeeping.'

'But, my dear, Thomas came to me with
most excellent testimonials,' said Lady Paget
meekly.

'Hang his testimonials. A pretty proof
of their worth he is.'

Lady Paget sighed, and went quietly
on with her knitting. She was accustomed
to little scenes of this character. If ever
there was any love in the baronet's heart
for his wife, it had long ago died a natural
death. He had married her, so he was
fond of saying, to provide an heir for the
estate. She, poor soul, having failed to do
her duty in this respect, Sir John probably
considered that his to her ended; but as a
man of his calibre must have some special
vassal to bully, he kept fast hold upon his
white slave, nor permitted her to wander
beyond his jurisdiction. She was a woman,
therefore she could be made to feel; she was
his wife, therefore she must submit. Quite

the old canons of civilised married life, but lately there seems to have been an upheaval in society. Women have dared to claim some freedom and some equality, have dared to assert that they may have rights and a soul apart from their marital lords. It is an impertinence, no doubt, an overstepping of the good old boundary which man with his larger intellect and all-seeing wisdom laid down generations ago, but the outworks are giving way, and the stream still runs on, making a new and wider course for itself. Poor Lady Paget rolling up her work preparatory to playing backgammon later on, was sadly behind the times.

'Shall I play?' suggested Connisterre good-naturedly. He loathed the game, but he loathed also to see a woman bullied.

'No, thank you; Lady Paget will play,' returned the baronet hastily. He remembered—oh, fatal lapse on Geoffrey's part—that once, some months ago, the young man, thinking only of the science of the game, and blessed by a series of lucky throws, had swept over the board and left him, Sir John, a loser by—let us not say how much. He would not risk a repetition. Lady Paget was shrewd enough to usually let him win, but sometimes, even in spite of her best endeavours, success would persist in dogging her steps, only to bring more pain than pleasure.

Connisterre resumed his conversation with Monica. He was trying to interest himself in her Utopian schemes for a general reclamation of the Forest Deane sinners. He was a philanthropist, too, in his own small way, but Monica's ideas were so vast and far-reaching that, coupled with her majestic superiority over human weakness, they rather took his breath away.

'That is so, no doubt,' he agreed, after listening to a fine peroration upon the laxity of the working-classes with regard to church-going; 'but if we are to reform or regenerate a man, we must first of all make him a reasoning, self-respecting being, don't you see ? '

' I see that they should be compelled to attend divine service, or be punished, as was formerly the case,' said Miss Paget.

' I don't agree with you. The perpetual fear of a rod will never serve to keep a man straight, for there is just the chance it may swerve aside, just the chance one may get past in the nick of time. You cannot *drive* a man to morality and Heaven if he does not chose to go, and it has never been proved yet that compulsory church-going did do any one good. You may hammer the Bible and the devil in side by side if you are not careful.'

' Indeed,' said Monica coldly. ' That is a sweeping statement, Mr. Connisterre.'

' Not a bit of it. Until you have made a man see that it is neither consistent with self-respect nor decency, nor, to put it on higher grounds, his reason as an intelligent animal, to wander about the roads drinking, loafing, cock-fighting, and the worse when he has responsibilities to perform and a stàndard up to which he should live, you will never make him swallow religion simply because it *is* religion. You must bring him to see the force and beauty of it first; later on he will take it as a food. It is no use putting a man into a picture gallery with his eyes bandaged.'

'But how are you to unbandage their eyes?' asked Monica eagerly. She disliked Connisterre's arguments, but was interested in her subject.

'Ah, there comes the tug of war. I am afraid we must each find that out for ourselves. You can't bring any hard-and-fast rule to bear on individuals. Do your best, argue, preach, exhort, with all the entheastic energy you possess; only, for Heaven's sake, don't bully.'

Connisterre had been speaking with some enthusiasm. It was a subject upon which he felt very strongly, but there was something in

Monica's face expressive of disapproval. He changed the subject at once, resuming one which had been discussed earlier in the evening, that of the possible removal to town during February of the Paget household.

'Father thinks that if he puts himself under the hands of Sir James Lockyer, the gout specialist, he may receive benefit,' said Monica, working steadily away at her passion flowers, which were nearing completion. Then she held up the work and surveyed it, evidently more interested in that than Sir John's sufferings.

'If I can do anything for you with regard to a house you must let me know,' said Geoffrey, diving under a table for a little ball of silk.

'I don't think we need trouble you, but it is kind of you to offer. We have partially arranged to take a furnished flat at Earl's Court, belonging to some friends of ours who are going abroad in the spring. The situation is a pleasant one and sufficiently central.'

'Then I may hope to see something of you

towards February.' After a pause Connisterre
added rather reluctantly, ' I don't feel quite
at ease respecting the little girl.   If she
really does not suit you, and you are keeping
her out of pure kindness, please don't hesitate
to say, and I will see if I can arrange something else.'

'Pray don't trouble about it, Mr. Connisterre ; Léonie is sure to improve, and in many
ways she is very useful.   Her chief fault is a
disinclination to take advice.'

' She is such a child,' he said as if in
extenuation.

'She is old enough to have been married
and assume a woman's responsibilities,' said
Monica freezingly.   ' Frivolity rather than
youthfulness might be laid to her charge.
You have heard nothing of her husband,
I suppose ? '

' Not a word *from* him, but, oddly enough,
I have found out something about him, something which authorises me to retain my
responsibility in her welfare.

'And that is—— ?'

'A distant relationship. Her husband is probably a half cousin of my own.'

'But I understood you had no connections who were likely to correspond with this missing man ?'

'I was under that impression also,' said Geoffrey, after a pause during which he was compelled to remain silent under a noisy flow of invective from the baronet, who had been ignominiously beaten off the field.

'It was——' began Connisterre.

'Your confounded luck,' broke in Sir John, sweeping the counters off the board.

'I was looking through some papers relating to——'

'Your stupid inability to master even the rudiments of the game. Any fool can win if he always throws doubles,' went on the baronet in a still louder tone, with an undercurrent of rumbling thunder.

Connisterre gave it up and looked across

at the players with a slightly resigned expression.

Miss Paget rose.

' Mother, I will take your place for a little time. And Quentin, Mr. Connisterre would perhaps like to go to the billiard-room. It is not very late.'

' Thank you, I should,' said Connisterre, rising with some alacrity.

Quentin rolled off the sofa.

' All right,' he said lazily. ' I will give you points and romp home a winner. Come along.'

CHAPTER XV

A MORAL DISCOURSE

We must not trust too much to happiness ;—
Go, pray to God, that thou mayest love him less !

JASMIN.

'OF all the cantankerous, snarling, evil-minded old sinners that ever sat on a magisterial bench or rode to hounds, that Paget is the worst!' exclaimed Quentin Lee when they were safely within the sanctuary of the billiard-room.

'He isn't sweet, certainly,' agreed Connisterre, chalking his cue with some precision.

'Sweet? He ought to be muzzled, the reprobate. If ever I get into Parliament I shall move a measure for the imprisonment or suppression of such men, the relatives to take out a certificate stating the impossibility of living with them.　Jove! what a clearance there would be, and how much pleasanter the world!　We could keep the nice, good-tempered, genial old souls to give a little ballast to the young.　There, now, wasn't that a pretty piece of play.　I told you I would cut you up as Mademoiselle Léonie would say—*Sans merci.*'

'By the way, where is she?' asked Geoffrey, consulting his watch.　'Surely they do not allow the girl to be out alone so late.'

'As I said before—at the Rectory.　Some elderly respectable minion will be commissioned to fetch her home shortly.　You won't see her to-night, for she is sent to bed at ten, as a rule.　Last night, however, she stole a march on them, and sneaked down to play billiards with me after the household had retired to bed.　She plays a good game, too, for a girl,' added Quentin patronisingly.

'Look here, Lee.'　Connisterre put down his cue and spoke with some heat.　'I don't know your ideas as to what is, or is not permissible for girls, but it seems to me that you were wanting in common sense, to say nothing else, when you permitted such an escapade.'

'How the deuce could I help it?' exclaimed Quentin in amazement at this angry onslaught.

'Help it? of course you could help it,' retorted the other.   'She is only a child. You know well enough it is not customary for girls to slip down to the billiard-room with any man when everybody else is in bed.'

'I know?'   Lee spoke rather sulkily, and made a fancy shot across the cloth. 'I wasn't brought up in a ladies' school, so how am I to know what is permissible for the female sex?   I enjoyed the game—so did she.   Nobody was any the wiser, and I must play billiards with some one.   You had better look to your laurels, Connisterre, I am going to win.'   Quentin made another stroke, paused, then said in a more conciliatory tone.

'It wasn't very late, you know—only half-past eleven. They go to roost so early here.'

'An hour more or less would have made no difference in the *esclandre* if you had been found out. I don't say there was any harm in her coming down to play billiards. The harm was in your taking advantage of her ignorance.'

'I rather like a girl with a touch of *diablerie* in her,' pursued Quentin carelessly. 'There has been one staying here at the Rectory whose attempts to get near the boundary line, without actually going over, have been lamentably funny. She wanted to be *risqué* and she didn't dare. Now Mademoiselle Léonie, although a perfectly discreet little person, has a pair of witching eyes and a spice of mischief in that pretty mouth of hers which are irresistibly attractive.'

Connisterre listened with a sense of growing annoyance.

'I think you have been looking at the

eyes and mouth more than was quite good for you,' he said with a short laugh.

'I don't know about good, but it was very pleasant,' returned Quentin, after another brilliant stroke. 'She is quite——'

'Look here, drop it.'

'I was going to say she——'

'Drop it.'

Lee turned round and looked at his companion. The amusement had died out of Connisterre's face.

'Of course, if you are going to cut up rough, I have nothing more to say.'

'I don't wish to cut up rough, but I hate to hear women discussed in a billiard-room, and when it is a woman with whom I am connected, I like it less than ever. Don't you be leading her into any mischief, Quentin. You won't have to answer for it to her—but to me, bear that in mind,' and then he turned the subject.

It was nearly twelve o'clock before their game was over, and the two men separated. Quentin, sleepy after a long day spent in the open air, announced his intention to retire. Connisterre was anxious for a smoke.

'I don't think I shall turn in just yet,' he said, as they paused a moment on the landing outside the billiard-room door. 'I have some letters to write. Are you coming down.'

'No, I don't think so,' returned Quentin with a yawn. 'I feel rather fagged. You are staying over to-morrow?'

'No. I go on to Carlisle by the 2.15. Cannot spare longer. Good-night.' Then they separated, and Geoffrey went downstairs to the library.

Now it rather unfortunately happened that this little dialogue took place outside Léonie's room, and Léonie, who was anxious to finish a certain enjoyable novel had set at defiance the rule of 'lights out at half-past ten,' and was burning the midnight oil. The evening had been a wearisome one, sapping a little of the colour from her cheeks. She had been unable to take an interest in the fact that this piece of charity print was stronger and more durable than the last, or that the state of health of the parish clerk's wife's twins, lately introduced into this world of sin and sorrow, left much to be desired. The fact she really grasped was that while she stitched and stitched as if for dear life in the prim Rectory morning room, Connisterre's brief visit to the Manor House was slipping away with lightning-like rapidity. Upon returning home Miss Paget met her in the hall, and dispatched her straight to bed, on the ground that it was already after ten.

Mr. Connisterre? Oh, she could not see him to-night. He was in the billiard-room with Mr. Lee; so with keen resentment in her heart Léonie had gone upstairs to bed. These few chance words exchanged outside her door, and distinctly audible within, came as a decided shock. Going away so early to-morrow! Why, that meant any interview she could have with him would be of the briefest. Morning was always Léonie's busy time, and she had no hope that Miss Paget would absolve her from any of her accustomed duties in order to give her an opportunity of talking to Mr. Connisterre. Without waiting to think further, acting as usual upon impulse, Léonie threw down her book, and forgetful that she had exchanged her serge dress for a flannel wrapper, and that her hair was hanging in a Gretchen-like plait down her back, she followed Connisterre quickly downstairs. The Manor House was a queer rambling old building of no particular architecture, and with a disregard of the usual arrangement of rooms. Miss Paget grumbled a great deal about its inconvenience, but to Léonie the house was a huge delight. She revelled in its low-ceiled, picturesque rooms, its winding passages, and occasional steps ; but there are times when even the quaint and artistic may have their disadvantages, and the present was one of them. Léonie spent some time unsuccessfully searching for her quarry, the reason for which was that Connisterre had gone first to the library, then suddenly re-

membering there was a certain book on art
which he wished to consult before writing
his letter, left it by another door for the
smoke-room, where he imagined the volume
to be. Not finding it here, he pursued his
way to the drawing-room, and spent a few
minutes there searching amongst the periodi-
cals and albums. Finally rewarded with
success, he returned to the library and settled
down to his letters. Not for long, though.
Startled by the noise of a door opening he
looked up, to see a little white-clad apparition
half a dozen yards away regarding him with
a pair of dancing eyes which shone like stars
under the curly hair.

'I have found you at last,' exclaimed
Léonie with infinite glee, as she made a rush
across the room to him. 'I was afraid I
would never see you at all, for Miss Paget
would not let me come to the billiard-room.
I heard you say you were leaving quite
early to-morrow, and then I thought I will
go straight away and find him now; but

when I came to the library, no, you were not there, nor the smoke-room, nor the drawing-room ; you had, as Mr. Quentin says, done a slope ; but I have found you, I have found you, and that is the great thing.'

All this hurried out in a breathless, delighted voice, with Léonie's two little brown hands holding Connisterre's in a warm clasp, her mischievous face rippling over with smiles and blushes, her whole aspect one of genuine welcome and delight. Geoffrey would have been less than a man if he had failed to feel flattered or appreciate it, but all the same he cast an apprehensive glance at the half-open door and Léonie's *negligée* attire.

'Are you not glad to see me ?' she went on in a slightly reproachful voice, as he did not speak. 'I have been so good. I have not made myself troublesome by writing letters to you, and I am, oh, *so—so—so* pleased to see *you*.'

'My dear child, why yes, of course,' he

responded, looking down upon her as they stood together in the soft lamp-light. 'I was sorry you were out to-night, but in any case we should have met in the morning. Léonie, do you know I am going to scold you?'

'But why?' she asked, with sweet astonished eyes.

'You should not run about the house like this,' touching her white dressing-gown and tumbled hair.

'I forgot,' she said, colouring a little now that she understood him, and speaking more soberly. 'I was so anxious to see you that I did not wait to think a minute; but it is pretty,' looking at her gown with the innocent vanity of a child.

'H'm,' thought Connisterre, with a thrill of vexation. 'I wonder if she wears this when she runs down to play billiards with Quentin. I must talk seriously to her.' But under such circumstances it is not easy to be serious. The witchery of the hour and the position was too potent, and Connisterre was no prig. He had too susceptible a nature to come uninfluenced out of a temptation like this, and was conscious of a strong desire to prolong the interview, even though he knew it to be unwise. His vanity was tickled by the girl's unassumed delight at seeing him ; the part of mentor was in this case a pleasant one to play. There were all the elements of a strong flirtation ready to hand, and yet——

'Look here,' he said, giving her a gentle little push. 'Get away to bed, Léonie. Do you know how late it is ?'

'Not so very late. Only twelve.'

'Quite late enough if any one should hear our voices and come down to investigate. You must go. Besides, I have letters to write. Oh, confound it,' under his breath, 'here is somebody ! What the deuce am I to do ?'

Léonie also had heard a step upon the stairs and stood still, a lovely colour coming and going in her cheeks. At that moment she looked more womanly, less like an irresponsible child than Connisterre had ever seen her.

'Hide yourself,' he said in a quick, excited whisper, and a second later knew that the advice was ill judged. Far better to face out such a situation.

Léonie made a dart away from him, but there was no time to reach the further door. She vanished within the heavy curtains screening one of the windows, while Connisterre, his heart beating unpleasantly fast, picked up the discarded book, and when Sir John entered was apparently immersed in its contents.

'So it is you who are making such a confounded row that an old man cannot get a wink of sleep,' said the baronet testily. 'I wondered what the devil was up.'

'I am sorry to have disturbed you,' replied Geoffrey, his eyes roaming with horrid fascination towards a certain corner in the room. 'The fact is my—my head ached; I mean I had letters to write, so stayed down for an hour or two.' He jerked out the words confusedly, but the baronet was gazing with a stony stare at the further window. Léonie, in order to screen herself from view, had drawn one of the curtains away from the centre. Part of the glass was uncovered, revealing the pale face of the distant moon.

'It passes creation that any one should be so pestered with an infernal thick-headed army of servants as I am,' foamed Sir John, putting down his candle as he pointed to the un-shuttered window. 'Look at that, look at that, I say. If their disobedience isn't enough to drive a man into the asylum.' At that moment he looked ready for one. His face was purple with rage. 'If I have said once that I *will* have every window shuttered at dusk, I have said it a hundred times. As if there were not burglaries enough in the country without a premium being offered to people to break into your house. It is that lazy rascal Thomas. I have half a mind to ring him out of bed to shutter that window. He would remember in future.'

Sir John's hand was upon the bell. In another moment such a peal would have resounded through the house as to bring the whole regiment of servants to the fore.

'I will see to the window; let me do it,' exclaimed Connisterre, starting up in a perfect agony of apprehension, while actual beads of perspiration stood upon his forehead. Good heavens, what a horrid scandal he had to avert! 'Don't you trouble, Sir John. I assure you I can do it. Yes, servants are fools, of course—all servants are.'

'Sure you know how, eh?' asked the old man, with his hand still on the bell. 'I won't have any risks run.'

'Quite sure.' Connisterre was already at the window swinging the shutter forward with a noisy clatter. 'For heaven's sake, Léonie, keep still,' he whispered, and cowed by something in his tone, she did keep still,

even though Connisterre stumbled acciden-
tally upon her foot, and sent a quick thrill of
pain through every nerve. But the danger
of discovery had been averted.

Sir John, after another growl, and a broad
hint to Connisterre that it would be a favour
if he would retire to rest, and allow other
people to do the same, left the room, and
they heard his heavy step plodding up, stair
by stair, until it died away into silence.
Connisterre drew a long breath of relief.

'Come, Léonie,' he said, gripping her
almost angrily by the shoulder as she
emerged from her retreat, so incensed was
he at the thought of their mutual danger.
'I hope you understand what a risk you
have been running. Never do such a thing
again.'

'But how was I to know he would come
down?' she said with a pout, her eyes like
twin stars in the small, pale face.

'How were you to know he wouldn't?'
retorted Geoffrey. 'Go to bed at once.'

She turned away from him, went half across the room, finally came back and stood by his side hesitatingly.

'Please say good-night, Mr. Connisterre,' she said wistfully. 'I am sorry I have vexed you, but really I did not know it was wrong.'

Geoffrey's face relaxed. He was only flesh and blood after all, and as she stood there in her simplicity, raising a rather frightened face to his, one hand playing nervously with the ribbon at her waist, he felt his pulses thrill, and a mad temptation seize him to take her in his arms and kiss the tremor from her lips. It was only a temporary weakness—the witchery of the hour, the lonely room, and the silence around them. He resisted it, but the colour rose to his face. 'I am not angry,' he said, taking her hands in a friendly clasp. 'Only, Léonie, the world has a very wicked tongue; don't you give it any occasion to wag against you. Goodnight; I shall see you in the morning.'

As the little white-clad form vanished

from his sight, Geoffrey threw himself into a chair, resting his head upon his hand. The letters were completely forgotten.

'I *must* find that man,' he muttered at last. 'Must make him come forward and accept his responsibilities, or there will be the very mischief to pay.'

CHAPTER XVI

IN THE WOOD

No man is so foolish, but may give another good counsel some-times.—BEN JONSON.

A DREARY looking morning, dreary by virtue of the grayness of the skies, and the damp, humid look which a night of heavy rain produces in late October. It had cleared during the early hours of dawn, but the ground was wet and sodden. Rain-drops glistened on the grass and on the stable roof; they hung pendant to the water-spouts and the shivering trees, which now and then shook themselves irritably, as if the touch were distasteful to their bare branches. Away in the east a faint pale line of light made a jagged rent across the monotonous gray sky which otherwise looked dreary in the extreme. A low whistle of the wind sometimes broke the silence, rising now to a scream, or sinking again into a dull, disquiet murmur. Not by any means an inviting or desirable morning for a walk, but Connisterre, who had spent a disturbed night, walked rapidly down the avenue, heedless of the inclement weather. It was a relief to be out in the fresh air, even if that air were raw and chilly. Turning sharply off to the right by a little path which he remembered of old, Geoffrey came at last to a low, park fence separating the avenue from the wood. Vaulting over this into the dusky recesses beyond, he walked on more slowly, for it was comparatively sheltered here. Some of the trees had lost their glory of gold and scarlet, but a few, more hardy than the rest, still held with a tenacious grip the mantles which months ago spring had cast upon their shoulders. Geoffrey threw back his head and stared at the leafy fretwork above him, through which the gray sky gazed down with a dreary

visage. A silence almost deathlike reigned
here in the heart of the wood. It was a
beautiful spot in summer, a lonely one in
winter, and at present seemed tenanted
only by Connisterre and the scurrying fleet-
footed rabbits. He paused to light a cigar,
and was fancying himself quite alone, when
there came floating towards him on the wings
of the breeze the refrain of a song, mingled
with a creaking, cracking sound, the origin of
which he could not at first determine. Connisterre listened intently. It came again, this
time louder, more distinct, and he recognised
both the singer's voice and the melody. A
quaint little negro doggerel, infinitely pathetic.

'I suppose " Home, Sweet Home," and
" Way down upon de Suwannee Riber " have
very much in common,' he laughed, walking
on. And so surely they have. Rich or
poor, wise or simple, black or white, deep
down in those wayward hearts of ours lies
the common emotion of humanity, a simple
natural love of home and all its old associa-

tions.   We may smother it, we may choke it
down, laugh, ridicule, and sneer, but for all
that the hidden chord is there in most of us,
and when we are old or weary or in pain and
grief from the world's hard buffetings, it is
strong enough to draw us back for shelter
and consolation.   So now in the dreary
silence of the morning the old refrain of—

> Way down upon de Suwannee Riber

came home to Connisterre with an added
touch of pathos, as he remembered the lonely,
friendless condition of the little singer.

> When I was playin' wid my brudder
>> Happy was I.
> O take me to my kind ole mudder,
>> Dar let me lib and die.

A pause, and more of that curious creaking, then the voice rose again, a clear, childish,
not very strong voice.

> Eberywhere I roam,
>> O darkeys, how my heart grows weary,
> Far from de ole folks at home.

Then followed a long silence.   Connisterre

put aside the intervening branches and came
out into the open.

'So I have found the nightingale,' he said
with a laugh. 'Where did you learn that,
Léonie?' and then he discovered the cause
of that mysterious creaking. The girl had
perched herself like an elf upon a low, naked
branch which jutted out some distance from
its parent stem, a gnarled and lightning-
shrivelled tree. As it swayed up and down
beneath her weight, it groaned audibly as if
in deprecating protest at having to work in
such an enfeebled condition. The scene was
a desolate one, but to Connisterre's artistic
eyes more interesting than a prettier one.
He would like to have straightway conveyed it to canvas. The seared tree stricken
down in the zenith of its pride by some
horrid convulsion of nature, the green-
sward littered over with thousands of brown-
tinted sodden leaves and yellow acorns, the
wide belt of trees a dozen yards away seem-
ing to encircle this little clearing in the

wood as if it were some hallowed spot where elfs might play, the dull gray background of an autumn sky sending out a voiceless dirge of the dying year, and quaintest of all, the little black-clad figure with wistful face and wind-tossed hair seated on the swaying branch.

'I learned it from Mr. Quentin,' said Léonie composedly, in answer to Connis-terre's query, and she shied an acorn at a scampering rabbit as she spoke.

'What else does that scatterbrain teach you?' Connisterre leaned one arm upon the branch, holding his cigar in abeyance. 'He is not a very safe tutor, Léonie.'

'No? Well, I do not care. He is amusing and that is what your grim English are not usually. I am weary of them, weary.' She tossed her acorns to the ground with an impatient movement, and laid her hand upon the rough coat sleeve beside her.

'Cannot you take me away, Mr. Connis-terre,' she asked piteously. 'Let me go to France or Italy, or somewhere that I can

laugh and sing and see the sun. I am unhappy, indeed; indeed I am.' She burst
into fretful sobs, which went to Geoffrey's
heart.

'My dear, if you really are not happy
here, you *shall* go somewhere else,' he said,
laying a friendly hand over the one upon his
arm. 'But don't you see any post in which
you have not complete freedom would be
more or less distasteful to you at present.
They are not unkind to you here?'

'N-o-o.'

'It is just this way,' he went on, pulling
his moustache with restless fingers. 'Sooner
or later we must all learn the same lesson,
the lesson of endurance. We cannot have
our own way. Discipline comes to us in some
form or other. If we were all free agents
the world would go to pieces.'

'But every one is not under discipline,'
said Léonie, drying her tears resentfully.
'Some people do just as they like; Mr.
Quentin does.'

'Mr. Quentin does nothing of the kind, except in holiday time. Do you suppose he would not prefer to be lounging about with a gun, boating on the Broads, or fishing in Norway, instead of grinding in a city office which he has to do practically three-fourths of the year? I have to work, we all have to work, and even if fate has put the silver spoon in our mouth, it is so coated with responsibilities that if we did our duty we should never taste the silver until we died.'

'But I don't want to work; I hate work, I hate responsibilities,' cried this young Pagan, in no sense impressed by the philosophy which Connisterre propounded. 'I want to do just as I like.'

'Then, my dear girl, the sooner you learn that your wish has no chance of being gratified, the better for you. Come, now, be sensible. Look at the matter fairly and squarely, and see if the present state of affairs cannot be endured until there is daylight in

the future. I know it is an anomalous position. I know you feel your husband's desertion ; but—and this brings me to another
point. Do you remember, Léonie, my saying
that I did not think he—your husband, I
mean—was any connection of mine? I have
reason to believe he is.'

'But how?' exclaimed Léonie, opening
her eyes in astonishment.

'I was looking over some old papers the
other day which formerly belonged to my
father, and have been left undisturbed since
his death. Amongst them I found one relating to a deed of gift of some few hundred
pounds to his cousin, Henry Connisterre.
Further search brought to light something of
which I had been ignorant before, namely,
that my grandfather had a younger brother,
a black sheep of the family. This man,
then, William Connisterre, was the father
of Henry, and uncle to my father. Do you
follow me?'

Léonie nodded.

'On reading through a packet of letters, I was able to piece up the story in part. William Connisterre had been sent abroad for some disgraceful act or other, and then probably lost sight of. Finally I came to a partially destroyed note, dated from Chicago, and written to my father by Henry Connisterre, his cousin, twenty years later, beseeching him for the sake of the tie of blood between them to send him some pecuniary aid.'

'But my husband's name is Gerard.'

'Exactly so. Mention is made in the letter of a child, a boy, but the name is almost illegible. It seems to commence with Ge——, so the probability is your husband and my half cousin are one and the same. That being so, it gives me a little right to look after your interests until he can be found.'

'When I must go to him,' said Léonie, with an odd smile. 'I do not think that would be nice.'

'But he is your husband.'

'He would like not to be.'

'Oh, well, that is neither here nor there,' said Geoffrey, flicking the ash from his cigar. 'A great many married people nowadays are in the position of wishing themselves celibates again.'

'I suppose I must live somewhere,' said Léonie with a sigh; 'but at present I feel just like a letter left at the post office—only nobody calls for me.'

'Poor child,' laughed Connisterre, giving her his hand to help her down from the branch.

'So it is "poor child," nobody cares a toss for me,' she retorted.

'Where *do* you learn all these expressions,' Geoffrey asked as they walked on side by side.

'It is that boy, that Mr. Quentin Lee; he teaches me what he calls the slang language, and it is very useful. Lady Paget wishes me to learn English quickly, so I am learning all kinds. Is it not better so?'

'Depends upon the kind of English, I should say. Lee's vocabulary is not quite suitable for a *jeune demoiselle ;* I wouldn't follow his lead too closely.'

'And why not, monsieur?' she asked, dropping him a little curtsey.

'Oh, because—because—— See, Léonie, there is something else I wished to say. Were you not playing billiards rather late the other night when everyone else was in bed?'

'Yes,' defiantly.

'Then promise me not to do it again?'

'But I like billiards.'

'Possibly, but you might like them at a more reasonable time.'

'Oh, les convenances, les convenances,' she said with a shrug of her shoulders. 'How am I to know what is right and what is wrong? Miss Paget will say to me, "Léonie, that is not permissible." Lady Paget says, "You must not speak to gentlemen like that ; you are too straightforward." Then, if I am not straightforward, I am equivocating. Bah, it is a funny place this England. Here it seems proper to do some improper things, and improper to do proper ones.'

'Illogical but true,' murmured Connisterre under his moustache.

'Do you know that we are going to London; your beautiful, dirty London, after Christmas,' she cried, suddenly turning the conversation.

'So I suppose.'

'Then perhaps I will see you?'

'I hope so.'

'And you may have found my husband?'

'I hope so.'

'Are husbands often lost?'

'They are often not to be found,' he returned jestingly. 'We have five women to every man in England.'

'Then there are four happy women,' she said with some energy.

'A negative sort of happiness some would say.'

Léonie stopped in the path, and looked up at him, a roguish dimple in her cheek.

'You do think you are very precious, then?' she laughed.

'Oh, well no, not precious,' he said, rather nonplussed by this rapid table-turning. 'We are rare, therefore not easily discovered; anything not easily discovered possesses a certain intrinsic value proportionate to its rarity, ergo — we are, as you suggest — precious. That is a logical deduction.'

'But I do not quite understand you,' she said, wrinkling up her brows.

They had come to the low fence which separated them from the avenue. Connisterre vaulted over and held out his hand.

'I will explain to you later on. Come.'

'No, I can get over myself,' she returned with some dignity. 'Please walk on.'

He laughed and obeyed. A moment later Léonie joined him, a long rent in the front of her skirt testifying to the incompetent way in which she had followed his example.

'It is too bad. I have never torn myself before,' she said resentfully. 'I wish I could wear a tweed suit and knickers like yours, instead of skirts always draggle, draggle through the mud. How do you think you could walk with a petticoat dangling about your ankles?'

'I should not attempt to walk, I should lie down and roll,' he returned with apparent gravity, as he looked at his watch. 'Do you know the time? It is half-past eight, and Sir John will be raving mad if we are late for breakfast. I'll race you to the end of the avenue.'

END OF VOL. I

Printed by R. & R. CLARK, *Edinburgh*

NEW NOVELS.

At all the Libraries.

———————— ♦♦♦ ————————

A ROMANCE OF DIJON . By M. BETHAM-EDWARDS.

JOHN DARKER . . By AUBREY LEE.

MARGARET DRUMMOND By SOPHIE F. F. VEITCH.

PAUL ROMER . . By CARRIE HARGREAVES.

MY INDIAN SUMMER . By Princess ALTIERI.

THE CURB OF HONOUR . By M. BETHAM-EDWARDS.

BORN IN EXILE . . By GEORGE GISSING.

THE GREAT CHIN
    EPISODE . . . By PAUL CUSHING.

THE LAST TOUCHES . By Mrs. W. K. CLIFFORD.

A TANGLED WEB . . By Lady LINDSAY.

THE PHILOSOPHER'S
    WINDOW . . . By Lady LINDSAY.

CAP AND GOWN
    COMEDY . . By ASCOTT R. HOPE.

UNDER TWO SKIES . By E. W. HORNUNG.

~~~~~~~~~~~~~~~

ADAM AND CHARLES BLACK,
SOHO SQUARE, LONDON.

THE
DRYBURGH EDITION
OF THE
WAVERLEY NOVELS.

*With 250 Page Illustrations, specially Drawn for this Edition by the
well-known Artists whose names are given below, and engraved
on wood by Mr. J. D. COOPER. In Twenty-five Volumes.
Crown 8vo, cloth. Price 5s. each.*

CHARLES GREEN	WAVERLEY.
GORDON BROWNE	GUY MANNERING.
PAUL HARDY	THE ANTIQUARY.
LOCKHART BOGLE	ROB ROY.
WALTER PAGET	{ BLACK DWARF.
LOCKHART BOGLE	{ LEGEND OF MONTROSE.
FRANK DADD, R.I.	OLD MORTALITY.
WILLIAM HOLE, R.S.A.	HEART OF MIDLOTHIAN.
JOHN WILLIAMSON	BRIDE OF LAMMERMOOR.
GORDON BROWNE	IVANHOE.
JOHN WILLIAMSON	THE MONASTERY.
JOHN WILLIAMSON	THE ABBOT.
H. M. PAGET	KENILWORTH.
W. H. OVEREND	THE PIRATE.
GODFREY C. HINDLEY	FORTUNES OF NIGEL.
STANLEY BERKELEY	PEVERIL OF THE PEAK.
H. M. PAGET	QUENTIN DURWARD.
HUGH THOMSON	ST. RONAN'S WELL.
GEORGE HAY, R.S.A.	REDGAUNTLET.
GODFREY C. HINDLEY	{ THE BETROTHED.
	{ HIGHLAND WIDOW.
GODFREY C. HINDLEY	THE TALISMAN.
STANLEY BERKELEY	WOODSTOCK.
C. M. HARDIE, A.R.S.A.	FAIR MAID OF PERTH.
PAUL HARDY	ANNE OF GEIERSTEIN.
GORDON BROWNE	COUNT ROBERT OF PARIS.
PAUL HARDY	{ THE SURGEON'S DAUGHTER.
WALTER PAGET	{ CASTLE DANGEROUS.

ADAM AND CHARLES BLACK,
SOHO SQUARE, LONDON.

www.ingramcontent.com/pod-product-compliance
Lightning Source LLC
Chambersburg PA
CBHW030758020726
47499CB00006B/1682